Folding her arms  hip on the arm of a ch stranger's extremely hot body. The taut drape of his shirt across his torso contoured ridged muscles and the short sleeve cuffs ringed nicely defined biceps. She judged his height at about six feet. His coal black hair was cut short Roman god style. His chiseled jaw— tensed now in increased frustration at the other half of the phone conversation—his chin cleft, and his olive skin hinted at Mediterranean roots. He redirected his gaze at Bree. His eyebrows raised as if surprised that he wasn't alone. And then his gaze dipped and journeyed slowly upward from her toes to a penetrating eyes-lock.

His extraordinary eyes bored into her— mesmerizing, pale gray with just a hint of blue as if reflecting the sky mirrored in the distant sea.

She gaped at him as her heart raced and her palms went clammy.

Continuing his phone conversation, he eyed her fixedly. "Yes, all right, Stan," he said, his deep voice clipped, business-like. "I have to go. Call me as soon as you make contact."

Still gazing directly into Bree's eyes, he pocketed his phone. "Hello." He thrust out his hand. "I'm Jackson Tremonti. We saw your sign. Do you have any vacancies?"

Bewitching Breeze

by

K. M. Daughters

Sisters of the Legend Trilogy, Book 1

Bewitching Breeze

Cover Art by *Kim Mendoza*

The Wild Rose Press, Inc.
PO Box 708
Adams Basin, NY 14410-0708
Visit us at www.thewildrosepress.com

Publishing History
First Fantasy Rose Edition, 2018
Print ISBN 978-1-5092-2251-3
Digital ISBN 978-1-5092-2252-0

Sisters of the Legend Trilogy, Book 1
Published in the United States of America

Dedication

For Natalie, Michael John, Maeve, Lilly, Colleen,
Maddy, Shannon and Steele
You are our magic!

Acknowledgements

Thank you always to our gentle, loving and gifted Editor, Ally Robertson for her skill and kind appreciation of our stories. Thank you to Joelle O'Shea Walker, our first Fairy Godeditor and sister of the heart. Thank you to our soulmates Nick and Tom for loving everything K.M. Daughters. And thank you to our babies for giving us their magical babies to love.

Prologue

1717—Off the Coast of Ocracoke Island

The Legend of the Three Butterflies

Hoisting her skirts up to her ankles, Sarah Binder Martin swept across the deck of the clipper ship, proceeding aft while the sleek vessel cut through the roiling sea. A smile played at the corner of her lips at the sheer fun of navigating the pitching floorboards. The vast western sky purpled as if God above inked over the canvas that He had painted lemon-orange, magenta and violet fifteen minutes ago at sunset.

She reached mid-ship, descended the steps and traversed the narrow hallway leading to the Captain's quarters. Her husband, John, the skipper of the vessel, shared his private space with Sarah and their three infant daughters. The berth was cozy rather than cramped—a togetherness that grew fonder throughout the journey from the West Indies toward Boston— John's new post, and hopefully, the family's forever home.

The floor rocked up and down, and then tilted sharply right and left as the ship rode the powerful swells on the course rounding Cape Hatteras. She hardly noticed, her body having grown accustomed to the sea's rhythms as if born to the seafaring life like her beloved John—and seemingly their triplets, also.

Sarah latched the cabin door behind her and peered into the oversized basket that the babies shared, observing her four-month-old daughters with keen interest. They cooed softly, kicking their feet, and gently jostling each other riding the ship's rocking motion. The trio returned Sarah's gaze, gifted her with toothless grins and riveted her attention on identical pine green eyes that sparked with lively intelligence and maturity. Sarah had learned since their birth that separating them in cribs brought howls rather than rest. The baby girls' angelic dispositions could switch to obstinacy as fiery as their flame-red hair if deprived of each other's company.

Smiling down at her adored children, she lit the lantern in the darkening cabin and then lifted first Maeve, the eldest identical triplet, into her arms. As she nursed her, Sarah marveled at her daughter's jaw-dropping beauty and wondered if this baby—or if her suspicions were correct, possibly all three—had inherited her ability to bind spells.

Cocooned in the ersatz nursery, Sarah fed and changed the babies. Anticipating dinner with John, she gazed into the looking glass and smoothed a stray red lock of hair into her chignon. The babies' bassinet reflected in the corner of the mirror and she spun around, alarmed at the wide-eyed expressions on the infants' faces that she had seen in the glass.

"What's the matter, my darlings?" she said as she approached the basket.

The babies eerily shifted their gaze in unison toward the porthole. A chill ran through Sarah as she raced to peer through the window and investigate the source of their fright. A blinding flash preceded the thunderous boom and shuddering explosion. Terror seized Sarah. In the glare of canon fire, she had spied the Jolly Roger fluttering in the wind.

Hovering over the babies, her mind raced. Barely able to keep her footing as the ship quaked and heaved under siege, Sarah gazed intently at her children's faces trying to determine if they could withstand her transmittal of power so that she might save them. If a daughter didn't possess the gift from birth, binding the spell would likely kill the child. The trio's identical calm expressions and the knowing gleam in their eyes encouraged her to try.

Overhead the scrabble of boots, shouting, screams and explosive discharges could only mean active combat. Wasting no time, Sarah leaned over the basket, closed her eyes and slipped her arms around the babies.

"Sacred Source, share my power with the precious three," she chanted. "In thy name and for thy miraculous purpose evermore strengthen their gift to bind spells."

The burst of force that surged through Sarah after uttering the incantation had her fixating on each beloved, animated face before she expelled a shaky breath. Convinced that she had done everything in her power to protect Maeve, Siobhan and Brigid from the marauding pirates, Sarah turned her thoughts to her husband.

Now she prayed that her store of spells hadn't been too depleted to help John. Grabbing the musket that leaned against the chest of drawers, she swung open the door and raced out of the Captain's quarters.

Poking her head above-deck her stomach sank at

the sight of the mounting carnage and the looming *Queen Anne's Revenge* tied on the port side to John's vessel. Her blood ran cold at the raging battle that the infamous, terrifying Blackbeard and his crew dominated. Taking a deep breath, she slipped up onto the main deck. Intent on delaying putting her powers to the test, she crept gingerly towards the bridge. Keeping to the starboard railings, she stole closer to the wheel in search of her husband.

Mortal cares and sanity abandoned her at the sight of John's dead body. Crazed, she emitted a howl and fired the musket in Blackbeard's direction. Instantly Sarah was cut down by a retaliating slash of a sword. As she lay near her love, close to reuniting with him in eternity, she glimpsed a comforting spectacle.

Three red-winged butterflies danced in front of her eyes and then flew over the ship's rail to safety.

Chapter 1

Present Day—Outer Banks, North Carolina

Sunrays glinted off the sleek, midnight black BMW's mirrored surface. Dr. Bree Layton slammed down the trunk of the rented convertible. She dragged an oversized red paisley suitcase toward the bottom of the sun-bleached wood steps leading up to the Inn of the Three Butterflies' wrap-around deck. Sliding her sunglasses over her brow to the top of her head, she tilted her face toward the cloudless Carolina blue sky, closed her eyes and basked in the sunshine. Radiating warmth toasted away the strain of the long drive from the Norfolk airport. She needed this time away from the Chicago gray skies as much as her parents needed her help readying the Inn for the peak season.

The screen door slammed. Her dad hurried down the stairs, his flip-flops slapping in rapid repetition.

"Wow! Nice ride sweetheart." A typical male in his car worship, Michael Layton rounded the front fender and ogled the luxurious car before embracing Bree in a bear hug. "But I could have picked you up at the airport and saved you the money."

"I wasn't sure when I could escape Chicago, and I figured you would get a kick out of running your errands in this little baby." Chuckling, she tossed him the keys. "Enjoy."

"Come to think of it there *are* a few essentials I need to pick up at the hardware store. I'll head over there as soon as I get your suitcase up to your room."

His crystal blue eyes twinkled as he hoisted the suitcase up with one hand and hugged Bree to his side with his free arm. "Between you and me, you're my favorite, Breeze, my girl."

Bree hooted a laugh. "Oh Daddy. You say the same thing to Skye and Summer."

Smiling, she mounted the steps at her father's side. He set the suitcase down on the porch and trailed Bree around the deck to the back of the house.

She drank in the pleasure of her first glimpse of the ocean this trip—dark aqua swells breaking on a nearly deserted, sugar-colored stretch of sand. A briny scented, gentle wind tousled her long hair and swept auburn tendrils across her face.

"Ah," she said as she exhaled.

Her dad sidled up beside her and stood silently as she inhaled deeply the fresh ocean air. Delighted to be back in her favorite place on earth she turned towards him. "It never gets old does it?"

"No it never does." The husky female voice emanated from one of the wicker chaise lounges.

"Summer!" Bree squealed.

Summer rose from her seat, opening her arms.

Bree sped over to hug her sister. "I love your hair. When did you get it cut?"

Frowning, Summer ran her fingers through her short, spiky, coppery hair. "Do you really like it? I regretted it the minute I had it chopped off."

"It looks great. You look a little like Halle Berry."

She grinned. "Bree, you always say just the right

thing. I wish I looked that good."

A cell phone buzzed in Summer's hand. She squinted at the display. Furrowing her brow, she said, "I have to take this. It's my boss."

"Let's get your things inside in the meantime," Mike suggested as Summer drifted over to the deck's railing, deep in conversation on the phone. "Your mom can't wait to see you."

He slid open the sliding glass door. Bree preceded him into the sunny dining area. Closing the slider behind him, he left her to retrieve the suitcase from the front porch.

"Mom, I'm home!" Breeze called out. She smiled as rapid footsteps sounded in response.

Barefoot as usual, Kay Layton rushed toward Bree, open-armed.

"*Finally,* you're here," she exclaimed, enveloping Bree in a warm hug. And then she held her at arm's length, her penetrating gaze unnerving.

"You look tired, love. I've been worried about you from afar. Now I see that I have cause. Is it your injury?"

Bree extended and retracted her arm while reassuring her mother, "Good as new."

"What then?" Kay persisted.

Bree pinched her brow and then scrubbed a hand over her face. Here in the Inn's homey atmosphere she was distanced from the recent unremitting stress associated with her profession as a pediatric psychiatrist. She had employed all her skills to prepare Toby and his family for his death. The cancer invading his tiny body had become a shared enemy. She had grown too fond of Toby, violating her own rule prohibiting personal involvement with a patient and his parents.

"The past few months have been so hard, Mom," Bree confided. "*But* as of yesterday, Toby's leukemia miraculously seems to be in remission."

"I just knew it!" Kay exclaimed, grinning broadly. "Let's go celebrate. I made some lemonade iced tea..."

"Whoa," Bree interjected. "What do you mean you knew it? Did you see it?"

"Hmm," her mother responded as she narrowed her eyes. "No, I don't think so..."

Kay gazed at the hardwood floor as if her thoughts turned inward.

"I sensed it," Kay continued. "The power of prayer. His parents must be ecstatic."

Bree gave her mother a warm smile. "Thanks for praying. And continue, please? Fingers crossed that he'll survive."

"I believe he will," Kay professed. "Come sit a while and have a glass of that tea."

Bree followed her mother's streaking trail into the kitchen, content to soak up the enveloping warmth that her parents had always infused in her family home like a giant hug. Staying at the Inn brought her peace. She relished the prospect of mindless housekeeping readying for high season. Maybe she'd find a little time for beach combing.

The kitchen walls were painted buttercup yellow with snow-white trim. Even when the hurricane shutters on every window shut out a raging storm, the room appeared awash with sunshine. Multi-sized glass jars brimming with starfish, whelks and sea glass lined the counters—the priceless treasures that her mother found during sunrise walks along the beach that fronted the property.

Kay yanked on the industrial refrigerator door handle as Bree propped her hip on one of ten wicker bar stools at an L-shaped counter. Joining Bree on the other side of the counter she supplied a tall glass of iced tea and sat companionably on the stool next to her. Beginning next week and all through the summer, the counter would display delicious homemade breakfast selections from six until eleven each morning, followed by plates of assorted baked-from-scratch cookies and soft drinks for the remainder of the day. Evening fare featured delectable appetizers, cheeses, breads and crackers along with complimentary wines that Mike delighted in carefully choosing for the establishment.

"What still needs to be done to get ready for the guests?" Bree took a sip of her tea. "Delicious as always Mom."

"Thanks, dear. I think we have most of the big cleaning done. Rachelle's daughter, Roseanne took a semester off from school this year. She needed money so Daddy and I hired her. It's unbelievable how fast she finished the deep cleaning."

"Are you saying that you don't need our help this week?" Bree asked. "Does Summer know?"

"We couldn't refuse Roseanne and we thought it would be nice for you girls to just have some unexpected sister time. Don't be mad that you're here on false pretenses."

"Heck, I'm *thrilled* that I don't have to help with deep cleaning. I feel like a little girl again on the first day of summer vacation." She touched her mom's hand and smiled. "It's good to be home."

"We still do need your help with cooking and serving, though." Mom chuckled.

"I didn't plan on staying longer than a week," Bree said. "I'll likely leave before the first guests arrive Memorial Day weekend."

"Actually I think we'll have early guests this year," Kay reported.

"Really? When are they coming?"

"I'm not sure. Maybe tomorrow or maybe tonight." She sipped her drink gazing at Bree over the rim of her glass, her eyes dancing. "How is that Dr. Steve you were seeing?"

Bree rolled her eyes and replied, "Dr. Steve is dating Dr. Richard now."

Kay's eyebrows shot up. "Oh my. You don't seem too broken up about it."

"I'm not. At least now I know what wasn't clicking in the relationship. Hey, but wait a minute," Bree said narrowing her eyes. "What do you mean you're not sure about these early guests? You know everything."

"Not everything, dear. I keep trying to make you girls understand that the things I see change all the time. People change their minds."

"Who are these guests?"

"A young man and his daughter. The daughter is having a hard time right now."

"Why?"

"Her mother passed away recently, and I suspect that the father is having a hard time, too." Wagging her head, Kay drained her glass.

"It's very sad. You'll be good for them. I love your take-charge attitude, Bree." Kay rose from the stool, rounded the counter, opened the dishwasher and set her empty glass on the rack.

"How will I be good for them?" Bree posed handing over her glass. "Are you matchmaking, Mom?"

"No, no... nothing like that. Here comes your father," she said swinging closed the dishwasher door.

Although Bree heard no indication that someone approached, a few seconds later her dad appeared at the kitchen door. Accustomed to her mother's "seer-side" Bree mulled over the prediction about the anticipated guests.

Her parents embraced and then Mike jangled the Beemer's keys in his hand grinning impishly. "Want to run some errands with me? Bree lent us her convertible."

"Oh," Kay groaned. "I wish I could. I love riding in convertibles but I have to make cookie dough in case our guests show up tonight."

"I can bake a batch of cookies for you, Mom," Bree volunteered.

"Are you sure?"

At Bree's nod, Kay opened a drawer, withdrew a laminated recipe card and held it out toward Bree.

Wagging her head in refusal, Bree said, "I don't need the recipe. I can make the cookies in my sleep."

She hopped off the stool and strode into the kitchen's work area. "Go have some fun."

Bree opened a cabinet, selected the dry ingredients to make the house's trademark, decadent, chocolate chip cookies and assembled everything that she needed on the counter.

"Thank you, honey." Kay bussed Bree on the cheek. "We won't be long. Skye is upstairs in her studio."

Hand in hand, Kay and Mike strolled out of the room. Her parents' love for each other prompted Bree's melancholy smile. Katherine Binder Duncan had married Michael John Layton almost thirty years ago and they still acted like newlyweds.

Bree dreamed of finding a lifetime-love like that and so far hadn't come close—the Dr. Steve and Dr. Richard fiasco a glaring recent example. Had her parents' romance set the bar too high? Was it unrealistic to want what they had and accept nothing less?

She put the first batch of cookies in the oven and headed outside in search of Summer. Finding her shoving her phone into her leather backpack as if preparing to leave, Bree pulled up short.

"I should go back to New York," Summer said reading Bree's perplexed expression.

Bree frowned, her mood darkening. She hadn't realized how much she wanted sister time until now. "Already? Didn't you just arrive this morning?"

"We're in the middle of a big case. I thought I could handle the paperwork from here. The DA thinks differently…" Summer scowled. "The bastard," she muttered.

"I take it things aren't great at work," Bree said.

"Right. I broke up with Gerald's son a couple months ago, and he apparently intends to punish me by becoming the boss from hell."

She raised her hand averting Bree's assumed I-told-you-so.

"I know, I know," Summer said in a sing-song. "You all warned me not to get involved with Brett. I should have listened to you and Skye. But I'm the stubborn one—remember?"

"*You are?*" Bree replied.

Summer gave her a lopsided grin. "You know what? I don't give a shit about Gerald's petty tactics. I deserve this week away, and I'm handling my desk virtually whether he likes it or not."

Delighted, Bree hugged her. "It's selfish for me to say this, but yay!"

"How cool is it that Mom hired Roseanne to do our work?" Summer said. "I can't remember the last time we had a week to play together like this. Mom even set up the twin beds in our old room."

Summer slung the strap of her backpack over her shoulder. "I'm going to run upstairs for a quick shower. Then maybe we can drag Skye out of her studio and go to the beach."

"Sounds great," Bree responded.

Her sister in tow, Bree opened the sliding door. As they neared the kitchen the scent of buttery chocolate tantalized.

"God, those cookies smell lethal," Summer remarked as she peeked into the oven. "There goes my diet."

She bounced over to the counter and swirled her index finger inside the bowl of cookie dough. Licking off the batter, she sighed. "So good."

"Go shower." Bree gave Summer a playful shove. "I'll bring some up to Skye's studio when they're done."

While batches of cookies baked and cooled, Bree sat on a stool, slid the rubber band off the rolled newspaper on the countertop and spread flat the local gazette.

Jumbo typeface read, 120 POUNDS OF COCAINE SEIZED ON CAUSEWAY.

Bree scanned the article and learned that shortly after midnight, a panel van had weaved erratically on the approach to the causeway heading towards the mainland. The possible drunk driving of the only vehicle on the bridge prompted the Currituck County sheriff to pull the van over. As the officer approached, the passenger door popped open. A man jumped out, scaled the railing and leapt off the bridge before the sheriff could reach him.

The officer radioed for water rescue and additional assistance on the bridge. After the second squad car arrived, the sheriff and three officers approached the van and discovered the drugs valued at over $7 million. The yet unidentified driver didn't survive the fall into the Sound.

Shaking her head at the unprecedented incident in her peaceful hometown, Bree took the last batch out of the oven. She distributed cookies on her mother's serving platters and then loaded a paper plate with fragrant treats. Opting for a tiny bit of exercise, she avoided the elevator and climbed four flights of stairs up to her sister's art studio in the penthouse.

Tapping her knuckles on the door Bree called out, "Can I come in?"

"Of course," came Skye's melodic voice, "especially since you come bearing cookies." Her laughter tinkled.

Bree entered the room smiling at the welcome sight of her sister in her lair. The pastel, sea foam green walls reflected the bright sunshine flowing through the wall of floor to ceiling windows. Skye stood at her easel.

14

Her waist length, russet hair was partially done up in a messy bun on top of her head. The rainbow-striped maxi skirt she wore brushed the tile floor.

"How do you know I brought cookies?" Bree asked. "Are you starting to take after Mom?"

"Nope," Skye replied without turning from the easel. "The smell of chocolate has made me ravenous for the last half hour."

She swept a brush across the canvas, a stroke of vivid purple. "I'll be right with you."

"If you're busy I can come back." Bree placed the plate on the wicker coffee table. "I don't want to interrupt you."

Skye gazed at Bree over her shoulder. "No, please stay. I'm just putting the finishing touches on this little guy."

Bree ambled towards the easel and took a closer look at the painting: the profile of a pelican, wings half spread. Skye's realism animated the bird as if he'd fly off the canvas any second.

"Oh Skye, he's beautiful. I love him. Can I have a print of this?"

"Sure. I'd give you the original if I hadn't already sold this painting."

With a flourish she signed her trademark S in the bottom right corner. Setting the brush on a palette, she wiped her hand on a towel. She strolled over to a mini fridge, opened the door and held a can of diet coke up in the air. "Want one?"

"Yes, thanks."

Bree fielded Skye's toss, popped open the shaken can gingerly and gulped some soda before she bit into a still warm cookie. Licking a smudge of melted chocolate off her finger, she wandered around the studio. Outer Banks-inspired paintings leaned against three walls. Skye's unique, three-dimensional style drew Bree into each scene. Dolphins frolicked in the ocean—so true to nature that Bree could almost feel the ocean spray on her face. Boats sailed silhouetted by a glorious sunrise, reflecting reds and oranges on the sea. Several portraits of weathered fishermen mesmerized her as if she could smell the tobacco smoke puffing from the pipes that dangled from their chapped lips.

"These are amazing, Skye. I want prints of everything."

"Where in the world will you hang them all?" Skye chuckled as she stretched her arms over her head.

"Trust me. I'd put up more walls in my condo for these," Bree assured her, plopping down into a cushioned wicker chair.

"I have to pinch myself. Almost every painting in this room is pre-sold," Skye said, her expression wonderstruck.

"Mom said that the art show in the Norfolk gallery was a huge success."

"It was fabulous, better than I ever dreamed. I met art dealers from around the country who want to show my work." She took a bite of a cookie. "These are sinful."

"It's wonderful that you're finally getting the recognition you deserve." Bree hopped up and toured the studio again, admiring the paintings even more at second inspection.

"Why is this one covered?" she asked pointing to a canvas draped with a white sheet.

"I woke up the other night and just had to paint it."

Skye strode over and joined Bree in front of the painting.

Removing the sheet, Skye placed the small canvas on an easel. "Do you know her?"

A small girl stood on the beach. The breakers behind the child loomed and frothed. The Inn stood majestic in the background. Three red butterflies circled the girl's head. The sadness in the child's luminous dark eyes stole Bree's breath. The sorrow and neediness Skye had depicted touched Bree's soul.

"I've never seen her before," Bree said. "She looks so lost and alone. You've never painted anything like this. It's haunting. I can't stop staring at her."

Compelled by the realistic portrait, Bree reached out and touched the child's hair expecting to feel silkiness beneath her fingertips.

"Why the butterflies, Skye?" Bree whispered.

"I don't know how or why," Skye said. "But the three of us are going to be a part of this little girl's life."

Chapter 2

Bree awoke before dawn in her childhood bedroom instantly alert despite her body clock's one-hour jet lag from Central to Eastern time. Her sisters' light snoring confirmed that even into adulthood, Bree was the sole triplet who faithfully joined Kay's sunrise beach jaunts.

Tucking under her arm the shorts, Chicago Bears t-shirt and underwear she had placed on top of the chest of drawers at bedtime, she tiptoed out of the room. She dressed in the hall bathroom and then slipped down the back stairway that provided access to the Layton family's suite in the Inn's main building.

Passing through the kitchen, she noted the popular items in Mom's signature breakfast buffet set out on the counter: baskets of flaky croissants and breakfast rolls, Danish, bowls of fruit, an array of dry cereal, a simmering pot of steel cut oatmeal on the stove and the tantalizing aroma of breakfast sausage casserole baking in the oven.

A lot of food just for the five of us. I wonder if those early guests arrived last night.

She entered the small-screened porch off the laundry room, plucked a bug repellent towelette out of the box on the sill and ripped open the package. Dousing exposed skin with the chemical-sweet smelling stuff, she glanced at the shoe rack in the corner. Three pairs of ancient gym shoes each had a sheet of fabric softener tucked inside. She smiled at Kay's attempt to freshen her daughters' stinky beach gear. Unhooking a Tarheels baseball cap off a pegboard on the wall, she donned the hat threading her ponytail through the back opening, put on her shoes and squatted to tie the laces.

The hinges on the screen door squeaked as she exited onto the deck. Rotating her shoulders several times to ease the stiffness that still persisted from her injury, she gazed at the sea. The brightening sky erased starlight along the horizon. She bounded down the wooden stairs and slogged through a stretch of shifting sand until she reached solid footing on damp sand along the water's edge. Ghost crabs skittered for cover inches in front of each of Bree's long-legged strides. Farther down the beach she detected a figure in motion and assumed she had located her mother.

Meandering, Bree soaked up the splendor of the pastel streaked sky, the wind in her face, the diving pelicans out beyond the breakers and the rhythmic pounding of surf on the sand. Up until college, the ever-changing seascape comprised the only world that she and her sisters had known. Countless fond memories had roots in this huge sandbar off the coast of North Carolina, and Bree missed living here—a sentiment that Summer shared.

Of course, Skye had never lived anywhere else but on OBX. Bree and Summer loved the Outer Banks, but Skye's soul belonged here. Reminiscing last night during the annual treat of sharing a bedroom, Skye had marveled at her sisters' sophisticated worlds living in the first and second cities. Bree's private practice thrived and Summer had many success stories as a New York City Assistant District Attorney.

Skye had encouraged her siblings to provide details about their "fascinating" lives without the slightest trace of envy or regret. Skye would likely wither and die if she spent more than a few days walking in either of her sister's shoes.

Although physically identical at five foot seven, one hundred twenty pounds, with fair skin, auburn-red hair and long-lash rimmed, jewel green eyes, the triplets had dissimilar personalities. Levelheaded, brainy Bree believed that logic ruled and chose understated elegance in dress and lifestyle. Summer's razor-sharp mind and single-minded valiance prosecuting criminals governed her romantic choices. She needed a man with depth and intelligence—a confident male who wasn't intimidated by her "awesomeness," according to Bree. Skye's free spirit, fearlessness and mystical power had routinely gotten the threesome in trouble throughout childhood.

Bree, Summer and Skye shared more than outward beauty. Descendants of the mysterious triplets whose legend involved The Inn of the Three Butterflies, the sisters possessed a higher intuition, psychic by nature. Only Skye, like their aunt, had inherited the full legacy of the legend. Soulful and quietly spiritual, the three loved with singular passion and longed to find a mate who could reciprocate love with equal intensity. Each woman's failure to achieve that goal had dominated the confidences that they had shared last evening during their reunion pajama party.

Laughing, Summer proposed a toast, "Here's to the Illinois legislature for legalizing same sex marriage. I'm sure Doctors Steve and Richard will be very happy together."

Bree snorted. "I just had a terrible thought. Since he's attracted to guys, do you think he dated me because I'm masculine?"

Skye and Summer cracked up. They quit laughing at Bree's doleful expression.

"You're serious?" Summer said. "You're a gorgeous woman and you don't even have to try."

"Right," Skye chimed in. "Your strength and independence adds to your femininity not the other way around."

Bree smiled at the memory of her sisters' unconditional love. She launched into a brisk jog along the beach sending clods of wet sand flying in her wake. Her lungs burned and her shoulder ached as she pumped her arms and accelerated into a sprint, catching up with her mother's lead in reaching the dunes that flanked the Bodie lighthouse. As Bree approached her, Kay lifted her head breaking her intense gaze on the sand, turned and waved.

Her breathing labored, Bree pulled up at Kay's side. "Morning," she huffed out.

"It's a wonderful morning. Look." Her mom displayed a Scotch bonnet shell in the palm of her hand.

Bree plucked the delicate shell off Kay's hand and inspected it. "What a find. Perfect."

She handed the shell back to her smiling mother who carefully stowed the treasure in a net bag. Emerging daylight illuminated Kay's creamy complexion, still porcelain thanks to daily gobs of sunscreen and her unwavering habit of wearing large brimmed hats. Lithe and trim in spandex shorts and a body-hugging top, her mother could grace the pages of a fashion magazine. She wore her long auburn hair in a side braid that hung over her collarbone. Bree's heart swelled with love and pride. Her fifty-year-old mother could pass for her sibling.

Kay pointed toward the horizon. "Do you have your camera with you?" she asked raising her cell phone up to eye level.

"Nope, but I'll use my phone's camera like you," Bree replied as she faced the ocean and checked out the sunrise through the viewfinder of her cellphone.

Rosy incandescence tinged the undersides of puffy dark clouds as a lemon ball sun emerged from the inky sea. Bree shot a few photos and then slipped the phone into her shorts' pocket.

Keeping pace with her mom as she continued down the beach toward the lighthouse, Bree joked, "So how many calendars can you make with your sunrise photos now? Into the next millennium?"

Kay giggled. "Probably. What do you have planned for today?"

"Since you surprised us with a bye on cleaning, I think I'll just be lazy—see what Skye and Summer want to do when they wake up."

"That sounds great." Kay halted and gazed to the right between a break in the dunes. "There's my lighthouse."

She pivoted and reversed direction down the beach. Casting Bree a mischievous glance, she tossed out, "Race you back to the porch."

Her mom tore off. Laughing, Bree broke into a run trailing her mother halfway back, increasing her speed with about twenty yards left to go. Edging ahead, Bree won the race with a noisy finish, pounding up the wooden porch steps a few strides in front of her mother.

Floating past Bree toward the water spigot as if she had strolled the last two miles, Kay said, "Pretty good since I'm nearly twice your age." She toed off her sneakers, stripped off socks, rinsed sand off her feet beneath the spigot and hopped through the screen door with energy to spare.

Too winded to speak, Bree took a turn rinsing off her feet as she made a mental note to add a sunset run on the beach to her to-do list. The injury obviously still affected her.

Ambling into the kitchen, Bree relished the cool blast of air on her overheated skin from an overhead vent. Wetting a paper towel she swabbed her face and neck with cold water and smiled as her mom deposited a mug of coffee on the counter next to the sink. "Thanks, Ma."

"Your sisters are outside having their coffee on the deck. But before you join them, can you please welcome our guest?" Kay nonchalantly stirred the oatmeal with a wooden spoon.

"Which guest?"

The pager on the front door chimed. She arched her eyebrows and grinned at her mother's precognition.

Bree strolled to the front parlor. A man clad in a gray and cream striped, short-sleeve shirt and slate gray cargo shorts stood just inside the front screen door. He steadily gazed downward, his ear glued to a cell phone. "It's seven PM there, Stan. Don't you think *somebody* would pick up the phone if you tried to get ahead of this?" he barked.

He clamped his lips together, furrowed his brow and continued riveting his gaze on her great grandmother's Aubusson rug, the only artifact of the original Inn that had burned to the ground in the early 1900's. Judging from the scowl on the man's face, Stan's response was less than ideal. As he jiggled a hand against his thigh in apparent frustration, he drew Bree's attention to muscled calves covered with sable hair.

Folding her arms across her chest, she propped a hip on the arm of a chair and appreciated the unaware stranger's *extremely* hot body. The taut drape of his shirt across his torso contoured ridged muscles and the short sleeve cuffs ringed nicely defined biceps. She judged his height at about six feet. His coal black hair was cut short Roman god style. His chiseled jaw—tensed now in increased frustration at the other half of the phone conversation—his chin cleft, and his olive skin hinted at Mediterranean roots. He redirected his gaze at Bree. His eyebrows raised as if surprised that he wasn't alone. And then his gaze dipped and journeyed slowly upward from her toes to a penetrating eyes-lock.

His extraordinary eyes bored into her—mesmerizing, pale gray with just a hint of blue as if reflecting the sky mirrored in the distant sea.

She gaped at him as her heart raced and her palms went clammy.

Continuing his phone conversation, he eyed her fixedly. "Yes, all right, Stan," he said, his deep voice clipped, business-like. "I have to go. Call me as soon as you make contact."

Still gazing directly into Bree's eyes, he pocketed his phone. "Hello." He thrust out his hand. "I'm Jackson Tremonti. We saw your sign. Do you have any vacancies?"

Rubbing her right hand on her shorts a couple

times, Bree stepped towards him. "Nice to meet you, Mister Tremonti. I'm Bree Layton, the owner's daughter." She clasped his hand lightly.

"Jack, please. May I call you Bree?"

"Sure… yes…of course." The simple handshake sent a sensual current through her and her thoughts scrambled. *Vacancies. Yes. Wait. Isn't he the guest Mom mentioned yesterday? Doesn't he have a reservation?*

"Um," she said withdrawing her hand. Her pulse skittering, Bree paced to the hall table and opened the reservation book.

Perplexing, the upcoming week was blank. "We're actually empty until a week from today. You can choose any room you like."

Glancing up from the page she said, "How long do you plan to stay with us?"

His phone rang and he reached into his pocket and yanked out the device. Gazing at the screen, he said, "A week is fine. I'll need two rooms."

He held up his index finger. "Just a second…

"Tremonti. Yes. Hold on," he fired off into the phone.

Jack turned his attention back to Bree. "Please forgive my rudeness."

His warm smile transformed his handsome face so dramatically that Bree nearly exclaimed, wow!

Radiating charm, he continued, "My little girl saw your sign. She seemed enchanted by the three red butterflies on it. Really excited. She…"

He huffed a breath. "We have a reservation further down the beach road in Nags Head. But she seems to want to stay here."

Bree returned his smile and picked up a pen. "You're both very welcome here."

She jotted down his name in the reservations book and then halted, the pen poised over the next line in the book. "What's your daughter's name?"

"Gabriella."

"Pretty," she said as she made the notation and then closed the book. "Where is she?"

"In the car." He spun around, put one hand on the screen door handle, raised his cellphone and said into the phone, "I'll be right with you."

Bree closed the gap between them and placed her hand over his, again experiencing a powerful shimmer of attraction. "I'll bring Gabriella to her room. You can take your call in the sitting area off the parlor."

Removing his hand from beneath hers, he gave her a brisk nod and then turned his attention to the call.

Outside, Bree fanned her face with her hand as she bounded down the steps toward the Audi parked on the gravel apron fronting the building. Her heart seized as she neared the car and found the passenger seat empty. Racing back toward the building, she barreled up the stairs and cut around the deck toward the beach. She braked at the back deck's railing.

A raven-haired child with her back toward Bree, sat in the sand. Summer and Skye, clad in matching, forest green bikini's, trod barefoot in the sand toward the little girl.

Chapter 3

Jack Tremonti rubbed a calloused hand over his scratchy beard stubble.

"That's fine. Keep me posted." He concluded the third business call he had received since he had arrived a half hour ago. His company, JET Computer consistently ran into the weeds during the rare occasions when Jack had taken time off.

He shoved the cell phone into his shorts pocket. As he strode out of the sitting area off the front parlor, the device vibrated against his hip. He retrieved the phone and checked the display.

Marcella again. Jack frowned as he jabbed the ignore selection. *Leave me alone Marcella. I don't have anything to say to you.*

Pocketing the phone, he continued pacing towards the front desk where a beautiful woman stood smiling at him.

"Good morning." He returned her smile marveling at the gorgeous women apparently involved in this family establishment. "I think perhaps your sister helped me check in a few minutes ago. A business call interrupted us and I didn't get a chance to give her my credit card."

He fished out his scuffed leather wallet from his back pocket, extracted an ebony American Express card and handed it to her.

The woman's smile bloomed into a wide grin, her jade eyes twinkling. "Thank you so much for making my day. My daughter Bree checked you in," she explained.

She swiped his credit card through an iPhone card reader and then handed it back to Jack. "I'm Kay. We're happy that you have chosen to stay here on your vacation, Mr. Tremonti." She reached out her right hand.

Jack slid the AMEX card into a slot in his billfold and then put the wallet down on the desk. His palm connected with hers accepting the handshake, and she cradled his hand within both of hers and shook gently, the delicate handclasp radiating a warm welcome.

"Bree is your daughter? Now that's hard to believe," Jack said, stuffing his wallet into his back pocket. "You don't look old enough to have a grown daughter."

He eyed the tight black running shorts and form fitting shirt that Kay wore.

She tilted her head, amused, as his gaze met hers. "You flatter me, Mr. Tremonti."

Kay chuckled as she handed him a pen and placed the credit slip on the edge of the desk in front of him. "But I have *three* grown daughters."

"Three? Unbelievable." He signed the receipt, separated his copy and slipped the paper into his pants pocket. "And please call me Jack.

"Where are my rooms located, Kay? Bree said that she'd take Gabriella to her room and wait for me there."

Kay handed him two keys. "You're on the second floor, facing the ocean."

She pointed to an archway. "There's a small

elevator down that hallway or you can take the stairs to the right of the elevator. You can also reach the second floor via the staircase off the kitchen at the back of building."

"Thanks." Jack gazed down at the heavy golden keys inscribed with numbers 210 and 212 that he held in his hand. "I travel quite a bit...maybe too much. I can't remember the last time I had a genuine key to open a hotel room door."

"We're a little old fashioned here. But I'm sure you'll find our service to your liking—very twenty-first century. If you have any complaints, you must let us know immediately."

Jack suspected that he had stumbled on the best accommodations on OBX. "I'm sure everything will be fine."

"Do you need help with luggage?"

"No, thanks, I'll handle it. I want to check on Gabriella first." He lifted off the floor the bulging briefcase that he had abandoned to take Stan's last call and paced towards the archway.

"What a beautiful name for such a uniquely beautiful child," Kay said.

Mention of Gabriella brought a stab of intense love. Smiling he faced Kay. "You've seen my little girl?"

"She's on the beach with my girls."

His conscience stung leaving his child with strangers five minutes into their vacation. "Oh. I better get her. I hope she hasn't inconvenienced your daughters."

"Not at all. My daughters love children. They have a way with them. I think you should visit your room, change into your bathing suit and join them."

Kay's soft voice and musical tones contradicted Jack's clear impression that she was used to being obeyed. Since the directive seemed sensible enough to him, he chose to follow orders.

He loped out the front door, descended the wooden steps two by two, lifted two suitcases out of the trunk of the rental car and then retraced his steps back inside towards the central elevator.

The lift opened on a tiled hallway. Jack rolled the two bags clattering behind him and inserted the key into the lock of room number 210. Pleasantly surprised, he surveyed the lime green walls trimmed with white baseboards and crown moldings in the spacious room. The door latched behind him as he kicked off his shoes and wiggled his toes in the plush dove gray carpet.

Jack placed his suitcase on the stand at the end of the king sized bed, opened the door connecting his and Gabriella's rooms and placed her *Hello Kitty* suitcase on the stand at the foot of her queen sized, canopied bed. A stuffed gray dolphin nestled between the lacy pink pillow shams on the bedspread that pictured sea creatures and shells. A ceiling fan with woven rattan paddles swished above the bed.

Gabriella will love this room. Well... My Gabriella before the accident would have loved this room.

Ruefully, he wagged his head. *I don't know her anymore.*

Gabriella hadn't spoken to him—or to anyone— since her mother's death. A parade of the best doctors and specialists that money could buy hadn't pierced his daughter's unresponsive state. They had unanimously advised him, however, that Gabriella's condition had psychological rather than physiological roots.

At home, Jack had used a variety of approaches to reach out to his little girl, from bribery to a one-time attempt at tough-love. He wasn't proud of having raised his voice to her, but her impenetrable silence tortured him. He pled with her to talk to him—even yell at him—to no avail.

His guilt probably pained him more than her muteness. Jack had planned to pick Gabriella up from her ballet class the day of the accident, but a conference call had run overtime. He had asked his secretary to contact his wife so that she could chauffeur Gabriella in his place. Jack hadn't given the situation a second thought until his secretary had rushed into his office a half hour later frantic to advise him that he needed to take the call from the police at the scene of the crash.

Jack had saved the message that Sophia had left on his cell phone beforehand. "Fuck you, Jack. I can't rely on you for anything. I'm done," she had said, apparently pissed off that he had interrupted her Pilates class or shopping on the Miracle Mile or tryst with...

Sophia hadn't minded the fortune that his dedication to JET Computer had yielded. She had loved their tony Lake Shore Drive address, her closet stuffed with couture clothes and her society status. She had even loved Gabriella. Sometime in the past couple years, however, she had stopped loving him.

Unbuttoning his shirt Jack ambled back into his room. He paced to the sliding glass door, parted the starched, lacy white curtains, slid open the door and stepped out onto the wooden balcony. Whiteheads crashed along the shore and a stiff breeze whipped his shirttails against his body. Open-mouthed he inhaled deeply, the moist warm air a salty tang on his tongue. Stress seemed to drain away affirming his hopes that this vacation might mend him and strengthen him to help his daughter heal.

Below he spotted Gabriella sitting on a checkered blanket near the water's edge surrounded by three animated women on the otherwise deserted beach. Female voices and laughter sounded. Jack focused on his daughter's face and did a double take. Gabriella beamed at one of the women.

My God, she's smiling!

Jack had labored the last six months trying to coax a smile out of her and these strangers had managed the feat in less than an hour. Thank God he had noticed Gabriella pointing to the three butterflies on the weathered sign in front of the Inn. As his mother would say, "It was meant to be."

Exhilarated by this seeming good fortune, he continued to observe Kay's daughters. Although two sisters wore revealing bikinis extremely well, Bree, clad in an oversized t-shirt and bike shorts, commanded Jack's attention. She tilted her head back and laughed as the sea breeze fluttered her gleaming auburn ponytail and molded her shirt to her breasts and waistline. A long absent surge of desire flooded his senses.

Captivated, Jack kept an eye on Bree while he viewed Gabriella's interaction with the sisters. Beach toys littered the area around the blanket. Gabriella and the three women sat on their haunches digging holes in the sand. One of the sister's hands flew as she sculpted a pile of sand into a turtle. His little girl wielded a shovel and added sand to another pile of sand where the outline of a mermaid took shape.

Bree gave Gabriella a hug. Jack's jaw hung open. He was positive that Gabriella squeezed Bree back.

Euphoric at the spectacle, Jack's heart pounded. He turned around and headed inside intending to race downstairs and join in playing with his daughter.

The phone rang and he checked the caller ID confirming that his sister-in-law didn't intend to leave him alone.

I guess ignoring her isn't getting the message across.

"What do you want?" He barked into the phone.

"Gabriella, of course," Marcella spat out.

"She's busy right now."

"Don't screw with me, Jackson. Tell me how she's doing immediately."

"I've had enough of your demands, Marcella. I don't owe you progress reports concerning *my* daughter."

Sniffling sounded as she predictably turned on the tears. Despite what he believed was phoniness, a crying female involuntarily evoked compassion in Jack. He didn't hang up on her despite his lack of affection for the woman.

"Please Jackson, listen to me. Gabriella is all I have left," she sobbed. "I can help her."

"If I thought you could do anything more for her than the specialists in Chicago, believe me I'd let you. You can't," he insisted his voice cracking.

"I can give her time, Jackson, something that you can't seem to spare for her. "

"You don't know anything about our lives."

"I know plenty. Sophia complained about your lack of attention every time I talked with her. Please let

Gabriella come and live with me. I could be a mother to her. She needs a mother."

Jack listened to Marcella's sobs dispassionately now, believing that her tears weren't genuine, and unmoved even if they were. *A mother to my girl.* The notion was preposterous. Marcella was even more selfish and narcissistic than Sophia.

"I know what my daughter needs. She needs her father. I have to go. Gabriella is waiting for me."

He disconnected the call hoping that the damned woman would finally leave him in peace, but suspecting that she wouldn't.

Gazing through the glass door he watched the foursome on the beach finishing the sand sculptures. A couple waded through the shallow water and shot photos of the sand art with their cellphones.

Amazed, Jack spied Gabriella squinting in the sun crouched next to Bree posing for the photographers' benefit.

After she had returned from her vacation here, his secretary had claimed that the Outer Banks of North Carolina was a mystical, magical place. He had attributed the description to her fanciful nature—but now, witnessing Gabriella's almost miraculous behavior, he reconsidered. *Maybe this place is magical.*

Despite his bravado with Marcella, Jack remained unsure that he could best raise Gabriella. Maybe a mother figure would provide her more than he could. Was he selfish keeping her with him?

Jack had questioned himself repeatedly, but he had to believe that he could provide all that his little girl needed. No one could love her more.

Bree stood, arched her back and stretched her arms

overhead. Turning to face him, she shaded her eyes with her hand and then waved at him enthusiastically.

He waved back.

Cupping her hands on either side of her mouth, Bree yelled, "Come on down."

Gabriella faced the balcony, a smile lighting her pale face.

Afraid that if he hesitated another moment, the spell would be broken, Jack hollered, "I'll be right there."

Jack tossed his cell phone into the room aiming for, but missing the bed. Slipping inside, he shut the sliding door. He opened his suitcase, located his swimsuit, shrugged out of his shirt and stripped off his shorts. Donning the bathing suit, he tugged a short sleeve Harvard t-shirt over his head. Jack grabbed his sunglasses and the room keys off the desk and headed for the door. As he turned the knob, his phone chirred and vibrated on the carpet.

Hesitating a split second, he dropped his hand from the doorknob and bending down, he scooped up the phone.

A quick glance at the ID display had him answering, "Yes, Stan. Is everything resolved?"

"All I need is your approval for spending and then, yes. We have mutual agreement," JET's CFO responded.

"Good. Email the figures and I'll review them."

"Done. But would you mind reviewing it now? I'm juggling a lot of balls here and your approval is critical."

Jack sank down on the edge of his bed. His head bent over his phone, he accessed his email and opened the attached spreadsheet.

Chapter 4

How long can he possibly take to come down here?

Bree wagged her head in silent judgment of Jack's apparent neglect and continued enjoying his daughter. Noting the child's frequent, expectant glances toward the Inn, her frustration mounted at what she perceived as an opportunity slipping through Jack Tremonti's fingers. She sensed that the smile the little girl had beamed to her father at the prospect of his playing in the sand with her was rare, and therefore precious.

Intense emotions warred inside Bree with every minute that Jack failed to appear: foremost an illogical disappointment. Surprised, Bree realized that she eagerly anticipated spending time with Jack, too.

Her breathing hitched imagining Jack advancing towards her shirtless...

"Hey Ella, what do you think of my critter?" Skye sang out, dusting sand off her hands while she regarded the turtle sand sculpture.

Bree's heart sank at the jerky head nod that the child gave in response to Skye's question. Gabriella stared fixedly at the ground while she listlessly sieved sand through her fingers. The kid had withdrawn as surely as a turtle within a shell, and Bree suspected that her father's lack of attention was to blame.

"You're calling her Ella?" Bree posed to Skye under her breath.

"She seems to like the nickname," Skye muttered. "It fits her."

Apparently undaunted by Ella's unresponsiveness, Skye continued speaking to her. "That's your reaction after all my hard work? Maybe you think that you can do better," she teased. "Let's have a contest. What would you like to make?"

Despite Ella's muteness and bowed head, Skye amiably continued conversing with the child. "Maybe you don't like my little turtle. I can create lots of other things you might like instead... A dolphin? A sand crab? A pelican?"

Skye winked at Bree, and then her eyes roved the vicinity. Bree followed Skye's gaze. The couple that had passed by earlier were mere specks in the distance. Since Jack remained absent, his daughter and the Layton sisters owned the beach.

"I can make a butterfly," Skye said rising to her feet. Ella continued to stare at the sand.

A wicked gleam sparkled in Skye's eyes. She gave a pointed nod in first Bree's and then in Summer's direction, closed her eyes and silently mouthed the chant.

Since age three Skye had demonstrated that she alone possessed the unfettered power to bind spells that she had inherited from generations of identical triplets in the Binder family lineage. Bree and Summer retained a heightened sixth sense and a visceral connection to Skye's awesome enchantments.

Understanding that Ella exhibited traumatized behavior, Bree wondered if Skye's mind-blowing magic would wow the child out of her funk.

Circling over the breakers in front of the little girl,

the red butterfly fluttered, ecstatic and free. In tune with her sister, Bree imagined the sensation of the soft wind beneath delicate wings and the breathless joy of soaring over the billowing waves. Kay had insistently drummed into her rambunctious daughter the absolute necessity to use her powers sparingly—"Only for good, and with very good reasons".

Bree concluded that despite Skye's best intentions, cajoling an emotionally fragile child into playfulness through spellbinding had backfired. Rather than squealing with delight and frolicking on the beach in joyous wonder, Ella shivered on the shore. The expression on her face baffled, possibly fearful, Ella shifted her gaze back and forth, apparently searching for a woman who had virtually disappeared into thin air.

Coming up behind Ella, Bree gently circled her arms around her shoulders and riveted her gaze on the butterfly.

Unbind this, Skye. She's terrified.

Summer's similar telepathy to Skye followed Bree's in rapid succession.

The red butterfly plunged downward and disappeared in the trough of a wave. Skye rose within the next swell, her red hair streaming behind her. Caught up on the underside of the wave, she stroked freestyle until enveloped by froth atop the crest. She shot forward riding the breaker, and bodysurfed into the shallows.

Unexpectedly, Ella spun around, flung her arms around Bree's waist and nestled her head against her abdomen. Bree stroked Ella's silken, raven hair while her heart melted.

Summer flanked her, her eyes soft. "Aw," she mouthed.

Sloshing out of the water, Skye approached Bree. "I couldn't help it," Skye said softly. "The painting. Surely it was a prediction. I thought I could reach her…"

Bree nodded at Skye and then gently clasped Ella's shoulders. Holding Ella at arm's length, Bree gazed into her round, crystal blue eyes. "I'm so glad that you came here today," Bree said. "We're going to have a great time this week during your vacation. We'll teach you to body surf like Skye just did if you'd like."

Hopeful that Ella would nod or smile or show some reaction, Bree was disappointed at the girl's blank expression and persistent silence. She shook her head and cast a frown at Skye.

"I propose that we divide into teams," Skye asserted, apparently regrouping. "Ella and me against Bree and Summer."

Facing her sister Bree said, "All right. What's the game?"

"A sand sculpture contest, of course," Skye replied breezily. She circled her arm around Ella's shoulder. "How's that Ella? Want to be on my team?"

No response.

"I thought so," Skye continued. "We're going to beat the pants off these two. What shall we build?"

Ella gazed steadily at nothing.

Skye hooted a laugh. "A great choice! I'm very good at making castles and I'll bet you are, too," she declared drawing dumbstruck expressions from her sisters.

"Yes, that's a good spot," Skye opined. "Where

shall we send them?"

Skye paused.

"Right. It's best that they can't copy our technique. Well, that's a good question…"

Skye stroked her chin. "How about the losers have to buy the winners a flurrie at Fat Boyz across from Jeanette's Pier?"

Skye grinned at the persistently impassive child.

Convinced Skye had carried the delusional conversation far enough, Bree furrowed her brow hoping that her sister would interpret her disapproval and quit the charade.

"Bree and Summer, please set up over there behind that dune," Skye directed as she pointed backwards toward a wooden walkway. She handed Ella an apple red, plastic pail. "Can you please fill this with water, sweetie?"

Ella trotted toward the shoreline providing Bree an opportunity to question Skye out of the child's earshot. "What in the world are you doing?" she muttered.

Skye held her arms out at her sides, palms up. "What do you mean?" she posed, her eyes wide.

"You know what I mean," Bree insisted. "She might think that you're making fun of her by pretending that she's answering your questions."

Skye beamed Bree a smile. "She *is* answering me. Honest. I can hear her."

Ella slowly approached, toting the brimming pail of water.

"Trust me," Skye confided. "She's communicating with me. I think I might be able to help her."

Bree nodded assent, trusting Skye's honesty.

Turning her attention to Ella, Skye said, "Thanks,

honey. Okay, let's get to work.

"Sisters, you have no more than thirty minutes to finish your sculpture." Skye handed plastic pails and shovels to Bree and Summer. "Stations, please," she commanded.

Bree and Summer tramped over the dune and then sank down on their knees in the sand.

"What do you want to make?" Summer said.

"Hmm…" Bree picked up a shovel and twirled it around with a few rotations of her wrist. "How about a whale?"

Summer smiled. "Good. We can shoot for quantity since we suck at producing quality."

Laughing, Bree jumped up. "Start digging. I'll get a pail of water."

As Bree navigated back over the dune, Skye protested, "Hey! Top secret over here."

"I'm not looking." Bree held a hand up along the side of her temple as she swept past.

She jogged to the water's edge, filled the pail and retraced her steps, again shielding her view of the opposing team's work in progress. Twenty minutes later, Bree and Summer sat back on their haunches appraising their dubious handiwork.

Three feet long and two feet wide, the "whale" spouted water through his blowhole via the four narrow ditches filled with water coming from the top of the creature's head. Other than that detail, the sculpture more resembled an oval blob with a fin than the leviathan of the sea.

"Hey, Skye and Ella," Bree hollered. "We're done. How about you?"

"Come on over," Skye replied. "Prepare to *lose*,

ladies!"

Gazing at Skye and Ella's fairy tale sand castle complete with a moat, a drawbridge, turrets, a walled garret and even freaking canons on the ramparts Bree conceded, "We have definitely lost this contest. Hurry Summer. Go step all over ours before they see it and we're *totally* humiliated."

"Gotcha," Summer replied laughing.

"Don't bother," Skye said. "All I want is that flurrie. I'm thinking M&M... How about you Ella?"

When the child beamed a smile in response, a lump rose in Bree's throat. Skye's whimsical nature seemed to work wonders.

"Let's go tell your dad where..." Footsteps thudded on the deck behind Bree drawing her attention.

Jack descended the steps and proceeded towards her. Ella raced toward her father while Bree, Skye and Summer stood in the sand staring at the man. Bare-chested, barefooted and clad in low slung, knee skimming swim trunks, he riveted Bree's attention. The sun gleamed off his oiled, broad shoulders. The wide smile that he cast at his little girl made Bree ache for him to direct that brand of delight at her.

"Mother of God look at those pecs," Summer said, her tone dreamy.

"I can't keep my eyes off his man-vee," Skye declared.

Bree gazed at the waistband of his trunks riding the vee shaped ridge of muscle. Her stomach tightened at the rush of attraction. What would it feel like to press her body against his, skin to skin? Heat surged through her at the prospect.

Absently she fluffed her damp bangs. "He's mine,"

she declared.

"Says who?" Summer said.

"Mom," Bree replied as the certainty dawned on her. Kay had seen some connection between Bree and Jack's unplanned arrival.

"Oh...all right," Summer said. "We know when we're beaten."

In motion towards Jack, Bree suggested, "Maybe he wants some ice cream, too, Summer. Let's make good on that bet."

Chapter 5

Ahead of the sisters' car, Jack swung his Audi into a parking space near the porch steps. Ella swung open the back door the instant that he cut the engine. The Inn's glistening windows flared fiery orange, red and pink reflections of the setting sun, an illusion of a blazing inferno inside the building. Through the windshield of Skye's salt-streaked Jeep, the evening sky vibrated with awesome color. Bree gazed at the beautiful display as she rode in the passenger seat.

Skye braked behind Jack's car, Bree and Summer hopped out, and then Skye drove to a lurching halt behind the palm trees that lined the parking lot.

A car door thudded and Jack sauntered toward Bree. Her pulse skittered as he approached. *What is wrong with me?* She shivered and shifted her gaze to her sister.

Summer dabbed a tissue at sticky ice cream smears on Ella's face. She huffed a laugh as pieces of tissue clung to the child's cheeks. Gently picking off the paper remnants, she asserted, "This is useless. Have you ever taken a shower outside?"

Ella gave a tiny headshake in response.

Out of the corner of her eye, Bree noted Jack's raised brows at his daughter's subtle interaction with Summer.

"You've never showered in the open air? What a

shame," Skye said as she bounded over to the group. "I'll bet you didn't know that we have the best outdoor shower on the entire Outer Banks," she bragged, her eyes twinkling.

Ella raised worshipful eyes to her apparent new hero.

Summer chuckled. "Um…and you substantiate this claim, how?"

"OK, maybe I am a bit prejudiced," Skye conceded.

She stooped down to Ella's eye level. "But I promise you this, Miss Ella. Once you take a shower outside, you will never want to take one inside again. Want to see what I mean? We've got soap, shampoo and towels in the stall already. I'll take you around back if it's okay with your daddy."

Ella shifted her gaze to Jack's face in wordless supplication.

"That sounds *awesome*, sweetheart," he agreed with exaggerated enthusiasm. "Go ahead. I've never showered outdoors, either. Let me know how you like it and maybe I'll give it a try."

Bree observed Jack's body language closely. His cheerful pronouncements to his daughter contradicted his furrowed brow. Melancholy emanated from his dove gray eyes.

"Thank you, Skye," he said, his tone clipped as if he could barely manage expressing the nicety.

"My pleasure," Skye chirped.

"I think I'll go for a quick jog," Summer said. "See you guys later."

Skye clasped Ella's tiny hand and then set off skipping. Playfully urging the child to keep pace with her, Skye and Ella disappeared around the side of the building.

"Maybe my assistant was right." Jack leaned against the wooden banister.

"About what?" Bree said.

"She vacationed here for the first time last year. When she came back to the office she couldn't stop talking about how this place is 'magical'."

"Of course it is," Bree said, her expression deadpan. "This sandbar casts a spell on you that calls you to return from your first visit on. Some say the magic is Native American originated... There are lots of legends."

Jack's doleful gaze bored into her soul. His smoky eyes, the hard planes of his face and his sheer physicality transfixed her. "Um... Just look at that sunset and tell me you don't believe in magic."

He shifted his attention to the western sky where the sun poised over the shimmering, iridescent water of the Sound, about to submerge and extinguish for the day. No earthly artist could duplicate the palette of the color-streaked heavens.

"You're right, Bree." The hint of a smile tugged at the corners of his lips. "Magic."

Jack's sweet expression disarmed her. His eyes softened as his gaze met hers. She wanted nothing more than to linger in his company and delve beneath the surface of this intriguing, complex man.

"Would you like a glass of wine?" Bree suggested, hoping that he'd accept, her intention to go for a jog forgotten.

"Maybe a beer?"

Jack trailed her up the stairs toward the Adirondack

chairs on the western side of the deck, positioned for ideal sunset viewing.

"Have a seat. I'll be right back." Bree slipped inside the front door.

She hastened through the hallway to the kitchen where Kay had set out on the counter goblets and several wine carafes. Bottles of beer cooled in a tub of ice. She scanned several labels and chose one of her dad's favorite brands of beer for Jack, popped off the top, tucked a glass tankard in the crook of her arm, filled a goblet with a purple-red cabernet and hurried back outside.

"Would you like me to bring out some cheese and crackers?" Bree handed him the beer bottle.

"I'm still full after you convinced me to try that sandwich." His hand closed around the beer glass that Bree cradled with a crooked arm. His eyes held hers as the back of his hand grazed the side of her breast.

A tremor zinged from her crown to her toes. Hyperaware of his magnetism, her gaze locked on his lips as he spoke.

"I've had pulled pork before but nothing like that sandwich," he said. "It had a completely unique taste. As full as I am, I could eat another one."

Amusement glimmered in his gaze and a smile played on full, compelling lips.

Her cheeks burned as she slipped into the chair next to him. "We make Carolina barbecue with vinegar and mustard instead of molasses and ketchup. That's the major difference. But we all have our secret recipes," she prattled.

Off balance, she gulped her wine, chagrined that she had all but drooled in Jack's presence.

He set down the unused glass on the deck, took a swig of beer out of the bottle and then scrutinized the label. "Damn this is good. Does everything taste especially good here?"

His casual conversation helped tamp down the unprecedented surge of lust she experienced near him. "Honestly, I do think that food tastes better here," she said. Warming to the subject she added, "Except pizza. Can't beat a piping hot Malnati's."

Jack did a double-take. "Malnati's? How do you know about Lou Malnati's pizza?"

"I know that it's the best deep dish pizza in Chicago, or anywhere else."

"Do you get to Chicago often?"

"I live there." She sipped her wine and angled her head back relishing the soft breeze caressing her face.

"You're kidding. Where?"

"In River North. LaSalle and Kinsey. My condo is in the Sterling." She gazed at Jack remembering his scribbling address information at check-in. "You live in Chicago, too, right?"

"Yep. And my office is off Wells. You only have a short walk from Malnati's on Wells to your condo."

"Absolutely. I usually stroll the few blocks to the Wells Street restaurant every Friday night for my weekly sausage pizza fix."

"Friday night is pizza night at our house, too. I'm addicted to Lou's sausage pie."

"I can't believe I've never seen you there."

He frowned. "We live on Lake Shore Drive. My wife wouldn't live anywhere else and would never eat in a pizza joint..." he trailed off.

Embarrassed? Angry?

"My secretary has always picked up pizza for me Fridays on her lunch hour. I heat it when I get home," he continued.

"Sophia wouldn't touch pizza—had to fit into size two dresses," he said in a gruff voice, gripping the neck of the beer bottle harder.

"Gabriella loves it, though," he said softly. "Or at least she did. It was a special daddy-daughter ritual every Friday night."

Jack closed his eyes. When he opened them, he averted Bree's gaze and looked off into the distance. He clenched his jaw and then swallowed several times as if to clear a lump in his throat.

Bree's heart swelled witnessing his struggle for composure. "It's okay, Jack. You don't have to say another word."

"No, I want to…" He faced her. "Gabriella hasn't taken a bite of Lou's pizza, her favorite food, since her mother died. I miss those times…"

Suspecting that Jack confided in others rarely, if ever, Bree felt privileged that he had chosen to share painful memories with her. Perhaps unburdening might dissolve the sadness that she read in his eyes. She touched his arm gently. "How did Sophia die?"

He flinched as if she had punched him. Regret pierced her and she wished she could retract the question, take some other course in finding a way to help him.

Jack kept silent. Remaining available to him should he decide to answer, she sipped her wine and gazed at the darkening horizon. The rhythmic crash of waves soothed and relaxed her.

The property's perimeter lights illuminated in the

deepening twilight while the silence hung between them. As darkness descended, she assumed that Jack didn't intend to confide in her further. Despite her attempts to blank her mind, confusing yearnings muddled her thoughts. She wanted to help Jack…console him. Embrace him. The attraction to this virtual stranger swamped her.

Still we hardly know each other. Why would he reveal something so personal to me?

Rising, Bree drained the last swallow of wine and set the glass down on the table between her and Jack's chair. "I think the mosquitoes will have a feast on me if I don't move inside," she said lightly.

"I should have picked up Gabriella," he blurted out.

Bree lowered to a perch on the end of her chair.

Jack stared straight ahead as he continued, "If I had, maybe… I was always pissed at Sophia. And she died pissed at me."

Huffing a breath, he lowered his eyes and fell silent again.

"Were you supposed to pick Ella up from school?" Bree said.

Jack shook his head. "Ballet class. Truthfully, I looked forward to picking her up from that class. I always went early so that I could watch her dance without her knowing."

He smiled. "Gabriella was amazing. Like a graceful butterfly. The other little girls romped around the room with no ear for the music or attention to the dance steps. But Gabriella focused on the teacher and mimicked her every move. She never seemed to notice the other students' chaotic prancing."

His tone rang with loving pride one second, and in the next, was somber. "And now Gabriella refuses to go to ballet class."

"Did something happen to your wife on her way to the ballet class?" Bree ventured.

"On their way home. Witnesses said that Sophia drove right through a red light. The semi hit her car on the driver's side. The doctors told me that she died instantly. Gabriella was unconscious when the paramedics removed her from the wreckage."

"Oh my God, I'm *so* sorry," Bree said as she reached out and gave his hand a squeeze.

Jack resumed staring off into the distance. "Sophia was a terrible driver before Gabriella was born. Couldn't keep her eyes on the road. I hated riding with her those few times that I was a passenger in her car," he said flatly.

"When we were first married I bought her a convertible—big mistake. Putting the roof down brought too many opportunities to rubberneck while she should have concentrated on driving. That car was in the body shop more than on the road. But she still managed to beguile me with a smile when I complained. It was easy to forgive her that…easy to forgive her anything…"

Snorting a laugh, he wagged his head. "That's when we still loved each other."

He drained his beer and rested a warm hand on Bree's bare knee. "Sorry. I'm sure you don't want to hear about all this."

The touch of his hand created a powerful connection between them as if their spirits fused perfectly. Bree sensed that she was *supposed* to draw him out and cement this unexpected bond between them. His face shadowed in the dim light, his gaze held hers.

On impulse, Bree covered his hand with hers and asked, "Why did you and your wife stop loving each other?"

"Hard to pinpoint. Our relationship unraveled as my business became more successful. She harped on me to work fewer hours, but fully expected to spend money and never look at price tags. I had to dedicate most of my waking time to earning enough to keep pace with expenses. Eventually, she took up with..."

Frowning he gave his head a shake as if to dispel the memory.

"I'm sorry," she said. "I shouldn't have asked such a personal question. But I would love to help Ella if I could. I'm a pediatric psychiatrist at Rush Hospital and..."

"What?" he spat out as he yanked his hand out from under hers. "So-called experts like you haven't done a single thing to help her since the accident. All you shrinks do is ask questions. How refreshing it would be if just once you provided answers."

Bree bristled at his harsh tone. "*So-called* experts like me? I'm sorry if I've asked questions like a shrink, but..."

She bit back the rant as the screen door swung open.

****

A dull thump sounded as the screen door connected with the side of the building, drawing Jack's attention. A burly man emerged through the doorway out onto the porch. He carried a wine bottle in one hand and an

53

assortment of beer bottles threaded through his fingers in the other.

"Great sunset tonight kids. Hope you enjoyed it." He bounded towards them and refilled Bree's wine glass.

Wonder if he can see how steaming mad she is at me.

"Thanks, Daddy," she said tersely.

Bree's father turned towards Jack and offered him his choice of beer. He randomly selected a slim-necked bottle and said, "I can't remember the last time someone called me a kid, Mr. Layton."

"Call me Mike, Mister Tremonti."

"Only if you call me Jack."

"Jack it is," he responded with a smile. "Hope I didn't offend, but you'll understand when your little one grows up. Your children never really age in a parent's eyes."

He tenderly ruffled Bree's hair. "No matter how old my daughters are; they'll always be my little girls. Can I get you anything else?"

"We're good, Daddy, thank you."

"Enjoy this beautiful evening," Mike said as he headed toward the door.

Halting abruptly, he spun in his tracks. "Oh Jack. Skye and Ella just raced past me up the stairs, and my daughter said to let you know that she was going to Ella's room and they were going to read together."

"Thanks, Mike."

Bree grabbed her glass off the table and stood as soon as the screen door closed behind her father. "I think I will just take this up to my room."

"Please don't go. I didn't mean to insult you."

She glared at him but stayed put.

He hadn't set out to alienate her, quite the opposite. For the first time since the tragedy of virtually losing his little girl along with his estranged wife, he had released some of his pent-up suffering through Bree's gentle urging. It felt good, and he hadn't felt even remotely good since he became a single parent. Plus, she had unwittingly edged out his debilitating depression just by walking across a beach or touching his arm. His overwhelming attraction to her was instantaneous. He sensed that Bree held the power to change his mind about the trustworthiness of the female sex.

"Please. Can I start all over? My frustration with doctors has driven me crazy. I was so sure that getting her psychological help would break through her silence. There is no apparent medical basis for her condition."

"What did the psychiatrist conclude?"

"Psychiatrists," he said emphasizing the plural. "They just pull their chins. Gabriella will not respond to clinicians *at all*. My sister-in-law is pushing me to let her raise Gabriella. She didn't think I was good for her sister. She's certain that Gabriella's non-responsiveness proves that I'm not good for my daughter, either. I want what's best. But I can't let her go..."

Overcome with emotion Jack bowed his head. Her delicate hand cupped his shoulder radiating soothing warmth.

"It's obvious that you love your daughter, Jack. Relax and enjoy just being with her this next week. That's what she needs."

He raised his eyes. In the dimness, Bree was a shapely silhouette framed by a velvet black sky pinpointed with stars. Frogs and night creatures chirped a chorus. The briny smell of the ocean mingled with a sweeter, floral scent.

"Is that your professional opinion, doctor?" he said, playfully.

"Are you making fun of me?"

Amused, he reached out and clasped her hands. "Not at all," he said.

Bree gently tugged her hands away. "Um...Okay. I think I'll turn in."

Jack rose quickly and again caught her hands in his. "Thank you for tonight. No one has listened to me for a long time." He brushed a light kiss on her cheek and smiled. "I think I'll take advantage of that outdoor shower."

Lilacs.

Her perfume filled his senses. "Care to join me?" he tossed out, fully prepared for her to reject the invitation.

But wouldn't it be a miracle if she said yes.

"No, thank you."

She strolled away from him, paused with her hand on the screen door's handle and then glanced back at him over her shoulder. "But I'll take a rain check."

Whipping the door open, she disappeared inside.

Chapter 6

Bree's tantalizing, departing remark played on Jack's mind while he enjoyed a bracing open-air shower in the wooden stall tucked behind a copse of palm trees in the backyard. His thoughts ran to cashing in on her rain check. Even after he closed the hot water nozzle entirely, the ice water dousing didn't reduce his hot fantasy.

Her drenched red hair cascading down her back. Her slim body soap-slick under his exploring hands. She hangs her arms around his neck and kisses him fiercely; her body molds to his. He cups her buttocks and lifts her. She wraps her legs around his waist...

Shaking off the daydream, he wrapped an over-sized bath towel around his body, tucked the edges in at his waist and padded into the building on the main floor, hoping he'd encounter Bree on the way to his room. If he did, maybe he could entice her to spin that fantasy into reality. But he didn't run into anyone during his trip upstairs to the second floor.

He unlocked the door and entered his room. The connecting door between his and Gabriella's suites hung open. Her room was in darkness so he treaded softly toward the suitcase at the foot of his bed. Unwrapping the bath towel, he slipped into sweats. He used the towel to dry his hair briskly as he headed toward the bathroom and then he draped the towel over the warming rack.

Jack couldn't resist tiptoeing into Gabriella's room to watch his child sleep. A profound peace enveloped him as he gazed at her angelic features. Her below-the-shoulder, black hair fanned out over her pillow, a mane of ringlets. He knew from experience that those natural curls were a bitch to tame with a brush. Since she was a toddler he or Sophia had to distract her with the "big guns"—letting her play with their smart phones—or forget about her sitting still long enough to gently detangle her hair.

He smiled reminiscing. It hadn't been all bad with Sophia. Not when they had sneaked into Gabriella's room like he had now to gaze at their slumbering child. Simple, innocent times. Before Jack's company had become a household name. And before he had left Sophia with too much time on her hands and had provided her with money to burn. Her betrayal hurt him deeply because he had honestly believed that his accumulating wealth made her ecstatic.

Wagging his head, he continued gazing at Gabriella. She stirred and rolled over to her side facing away from him. He propped a hip on the edge of her bed and gently stroked her silky tresses, content; as close to feeling happy as he had in years.

Just relax and enjoy being with her this week, the lovely Doctor Bree said.

Maybe that was what his daughter needed. *Certainly that's what I need.*

Jack leaned down and gently kissed the crown of her head. He rose and returned to his room, leaving her door ajar. Restless, he considered his entertainment options. The television would wake her. He rejected

58

streaming something on his laptop using earphones, having had enough of peering at small screens that day.

Confident that Gabriella would sleep securely behind locked doors, Jack pulled on a Polo shirt, slid his feet into rubber flip-flops, strode over to the door and soundlessly turned the knob. Out in the hallway, he locked the door and slipped the key into the waist pocket inside his sweat pants.

With no particular destination in mind, he descended the back stairway that led into the kitchen. From beneath the cabinets, track lights cast pale yellow colored pools onto the length of black granite countertop. The refrigerator hummed and a soft whir emanated from the air conditioning vents. The homey scents of baking lingered in the air.

Jack felt like a home invader in this private space. But Kay had emphasized her philosophy of hospitality, so he didn't hesitate to amble over to the counter, lift the glass dome cover and nab a chocolate chip cookie off the plate. He repositioned the cover over the plate of cookies. As he munched, he speculated about whether or not the establishment had a gym where he could pump iron for a while.

A basso chuckle that sounded from the shadows in the far corner of the room snagged Jack's attention. "Hello?" He squinted in the direction of the voice.

"If you want milk with that cookie, bring a glass over," Mike said.

Smiling Jack opened and closed three cabinet doors until he found the glassware on the fourth try. He strode over to the ice cream table where Mike sat presenting his back to Jack. The man gazed out through the window.

Jack followed his gaze. A glistening ribbon of moonlight reflected on the calm sea.

Mike angled his head to peer up at Jack and smiled. "Help yourself." He indicated the sweating glass pitcher of milk at the center of the table.

Jack filled his glass and set it down on the table. He pulled up a chair, dunked the cookie remnant in the milk and downed it in one swallow. Grinning he remarked, "Reminds me of when I was a kid. My mother always had cookies and milk for us after school."

"Us? How many in your family?"

"Would you believe eight? Three sisters and four brothers. I'm the eldest," Jack replied.

"Huh," Mike commented. "Me, too...of six brothers and one sister. Tessa. She's the baby."

"Well, this is an uncommon coincidence," Jack said. "My three sisters ruled us boys."

Mike hooted a laugh. "Tessa is a real royal princess who believes we were born to do her bidding. Obviously, my parents wouldn't quit until Ma had a baby girl."

"Little girls steal your heart," Jack said.

"That is the God's honest truth. I could never say no to my girls. Kay keeps me in check."

"You have beautiful daughters," Jack said, Bree foremost in his mind.

Mike narrowed his eyes. "I have tried hard to terrify boys sniffing around them since they were fourteen. Now that they're grown women...well..."

Jack chuckled. "I can relate. Gabriella is a beauty."

"She is at that. I'm glad you understand. Beware, son."

Mike's insinuation wasn't lost on Jack. Had he overheard his invitation to Bree earlier? Could her father sense his overwhelming attraction to Bree? "Duly noted," he responded.

Sliding a plate of cookies along the tabletop, Mike said, "She's out walking on the beach."

Convinced that the man was a mind reader, Jack confirmed, "Bree?"

Mike nodded assent.

Reaching for another cookie, Jack said, "I think I'll leave her to her solitude. I'm certain that I offended her earlier."

"How so?"

"I'm pretty disgusted with psychiatrists. Because of problems with my daughter. I apologized, but I insulted her profession."

"Hmm," Mike remarked. "She's an excellent physician. If she's willing to help, you might want to pay attention to her advice."

"I'll try, thank you."

"And she's not one to hold a grudge. She's a real sweetheart. If I were you, I'd be walking on that beach."

Jack smiled. "I really don't want to intrude on her privacy. Besides, Gabriella is alone upstairs and I can't leave the building."

"No worries there. We have the best security cameras money can buy," Mike said beaming. "JET ProShield Version 6. I love tech. Comes from reconnaissance missions when I was a SEAL."

"Did you see action?"

"Yep. Vietnam. Did you serve?"

"Yes. Air Force. Iraq and Afghanistan."

Mike took a sip of milk. "The stories we could tell, right, son?"

Nodding, Jack asked, "So you like my security system?"

"Yours?"

"Yeah. JET Computer is my company."

He slapped his hand on the table. "Well, I'll be damned. Of course. Jackson E. Tremonti. Jack is your nickname. Sure is a pleasure to know you. Every device from laptop to smartphone in this house is JET. Wouldn't buy anything else."

Jack grinned at the deeply satisfying testimonial. The hard work, the endless hours, the personal sacrifice all distilled into Mike's understanding Jack's defining purpose in building JET Computer—product excellence that deserves consumer loyalty like Mike's.

"Thanks, Mike. That means a lot."

"It's the God's honest truth."

Curious about Bree's family background, Jack posed, "So how does a Navy SEAL come to be an innkeeper on the Outer Banks? Is this where you grew up?"

"No. I'm from the Bronx. Kay grew up here. And so have our girls. I was stationed in Norfolk and a few of my buddies and I came to OBX on furlough. Loved it here. After our last tour, we decided to start a paint contracting business working out of a shop we rented cheap in Kill Devil Hills. Painting this place was one of our first jobs. I met Kay and I became a believer in love at first sight. I had to marry the girl. She had inherited this inn from family, and so the story. I'm still a painter."

"Easy to see why you were so taken with her. Your

wife is as stunning and lovely as your daughters."

"Helping raise strong, independent women, like their mother, has made me the luckiest man on earth."

"That strikes me as the God's honest truth," Jack said borrowing Mike's phrase. "I would feel exactly the same way about Gabriella. If she…"

He trailed off crushed by the challenges that he had yet to overcome with her.

Mike brushed his hand on Jack's arm. "It will be all right, son. You're meant to be here with your little girl right now. I feel it in my bones."

Mike shoved back his chair and rose. Jack noted the man's muscular physique surprised now that he hadn't taken him for ex-military.

"Come with me, son," Mike requested. "Something I want to give you before I turn in."

Jack stood up and fell into pace with him out of the kitchen, through the dining room and into the reception hall. Mike opened a desk drawer, extracted a trifold brochure and handed it to Jack.

"Here you go, Jack. Some reading material you might find interesting."

Jack eyed the brochure that depicted a pirate ship flying the Jolly Roger with the heading, *The Legend of the Three Butterflies.*

"Thanks," Jack said.

"So you know, my Kay has two identical sisters. For contemporary reference." Mike's eyes gleamed. "Since you're interested in my Bree, you should brush up on family folklore."

"Um," Jack stammered. "I wouldn't say…"

Mike brushed off further comment with a wave of his hand. "No need for explanation, son. As I said, it took me about five seconds to fall for her mother. I'm going to do some reading in my room. If you go out, be sure to bring one of these keys," he said pointing to a wicker basket on the desk. "They fit the lock on the front door. Night."

"Good night." Jack stood holding the brochure in his hand a few seconds. "Hey, Mike." Jack caught up with him before he reached the stairway.

Halting and facing Jack, Mike replied, "Yes?"

"Do you have a gym here?"

"Sure do. It's in the basement. I have a steam room, too. Meet me there at 5:30 tomorrow morning if you'd like a workout partner."

"I'm an early riser. Sounds good."

Mike paced over to the front stairway as Jack drifted back into the kitchen.

Since she hadn't appeared while he conversed with Mike, Jack figured that Bree was still outside walking the beach. The temptation to join her in the moonlight tugged on him, but his protective instincts as a father won out. Despite his confidence in the JET security system, he hastened back up to his room. *What if she wakes up and can't find me? The last thing she needs is more fear in her life.*

Back in his bathroom, he splashed water on his face and then brushed his teeth. Propped against pillows leaning against the headboard on his absurdly comfortable bed, he perused the brochure. *Identical auburn haired triplets, arresting pine green eyes. A battle with Blackbeard. Three red butterflies? The woman was a witch? She turned her babies into insects?*

Jack nodded off, wondering what the historical sci-fi had to do with his interest in Bree.

Chapter 7

Bree plucked a fluffy bath towel off the warming rack and dried her hair. The fragrance of her mother's vanilla French toast tantalized her. She stepped out of the connecting bathroom into the now empty bedroom, apparently abandoned by her sisters as soon as the tempting cooking aromas wafted their way.

The hot shower had revived Bree after a restless night. If only she had veered away from the outdoor shower stall before her head-clearing solitary walk on the beach last evening. She had spied Jack's bare feet and muscular calves below the bottom of the shower's three-quarter door, water sluicing down over sable-haired legs.

That cocky man. His invitation to take a shower with him, a virtual stranger, should have insulted me.

Instead, Bree couldn't stop thinking about her missed chance to shed her clothes and to wrap herself around his sudsy, taut body.

Twisting her hair into a messy, damp bun on the top of her head, she hurried out of the room, intent on devouring the breakfast feast.

The sun-dappled kitchen buzzed with conversation as Bree rushed in, hoping that the chafing dish was still full.

Kay sat at the head of the table. She beamed Bree a smile. "Good morning, honey."

"Morning, Mom." She kissed her mother's cheek and then drifted over to the buffet.

A cream-colored dinner plate in hand, Bree slid open the top of the chafing dish and snagged two pieces of the buttery bread.

"Back in Chicago I dream about this breakfast all the time," Bree said taking a seat at the table.

"Sometimes I think I can smell it when I first wake up," Summer joked, her mouth full.

"Where are our guests?" Bree liberally doused the toast with maple syrup.

"Skye just went up to tell them breakfast is ready," Mike said as he made the rounds filling coffee cups. He gave Bree's shoulder an affectionate squeeze as he filled her cup to the brim.

Cutting the food into bite-sized cubes, Bree forked up a mouthful. "Delicious as usual, Mom. Well worth the wait." Bree sighed as she chewed another bite.

Skye entered the room holding Ella's hand. After settling the child into a seat next to Bree, Skye filled two plates while chattering in one-way conversation with the silent little girl.

"Your dad will be down as soon as he finishes his phone call. I bet you're hungry. You will *love* this French toast. We three sure loved it when we were your age. We still race each other to get our fill now that we're grown up."

Skye placed a plate in front of Ella, took the seat to her left, and cut the bread into strips before tucking into her own meal.

Bree poured a pool of syrup onto Ella's plate for dipping and Mike produced a large glass of foamy chocolate milk for her. Ella cheeks dimpled with a quick smile and then she dug in.

Kay finished her tea and rose from her chair. She carried her cup and plate into the kitchen's work area and loaded the industrial dishwasher. "What are your plans for the day girls?"

"I can't get out of a morning conference call," Summer complained. She gazed at their father. "Is it OK with you if I hole up in your office for a couple hours?"

"No problem," he replied. "I just wish you didn't have to work so hard."

"It can't be helped. We're in the middle of a big case."

Skye smiled at Kay. "I'm free all day. Already finished my commission pieces." She spooned a second helping of fruit salad from a crystal bowl in the center of the table.

Bree finished her meal and sat back in her chair. "Any suggestions, Mom?" Bree asked as she massaged small circles on Ella's back, glad that the child didn't shrug her hand away.

"The weather is going to be gorgeous today, in the high 70's. Most people will be soaking up the sun. So you know my top suggestion."

"The aquarium," Skye and Bree concluded in unison.

When they were kids, Kay rounded up her brood on the sunniest days for a visit to the aquarium, shrewdly avoiding crowds. The majority of "mainlander" tourists sunned on the beach when the weather was clear, and only visited indoor attractions when it rained.

"There's an aquarium on the island?" Jack's voice

boomed as he strode into the room. "Sorry I'm late. Something smells great."

He grabbed a plate, piled on a generous portion and sat down across from Ella.

Wielding his knife and fork, he scraped a portion onto Ella's empty plate before he sampled the food.

Bree's heart warmed at his unaffected tenderness. *Being a dad comes naturally to him. Too bad he doesn't seem to know that.*

"The salty air sure increases my appetite," he said. "Last night I thought I was full enough for a couple of days. And here I am stuffing my face. Kay, this is delicious."

"I'm glad you like it." Kay filled his coffee mug. "And yes, we do have a wonderful aquarium here. There are brochures at the front desk if you'd like details. Skye and Bree were just talking about visiting there today."

"Sounds good. What do you think, sweetheart? Would you like to go with me?" Jack posed.

Ella had bowed her head since her father entered the room, hiding behind the curtain of her long glossy hair. She gave the slightest nod.

Jack's eyes brightened. He turned toward Bree. "Come with us."

His tone radiated authority. *Come with us.* More a command than an invitation. Even so, it held appeal for her. Jack Tremonti emanated virility and power. Attraction tugged at her core and set her pulse racing. Her professional instincts advised her to decline. She should encourage father-daughter time to heal the apparent rift between Jack and Ella.

"We'd love to go," Skye sang out. "Thanks for

asking."

She popped up from the table ignoring Bree's raised eyebrows. "Come on, squirt," she beckoned to Ella. "Let's go brush our teeth and stuff. I like to get there by nine when they open."

Ella's eyes gleamed as she trailed Skye out of the kitchen.

"Meet you guys in the front parlor in ten minutes," Skye called over her shoulder.

"Skye has a huge heart, but she can be outrageously bossy. If you would rather have some alone time with Ella, I understand. You won't hurt our feelings, I promise." Bree touched his arm gently, stunned by a rush of sheer animal magnetism.

Jack's eyes held hers. "I want alone time with *you*. Perhaps tonight?"

Pinned by his smoldering gaze, Bree's cheeks flamed and a shiver ran through her. "We'll see," she said softly. "About the aquarium…?"

"Gabriella hangs on Skye's every word and she seems happy in your company," Jack said. "So am I," he added evenly.

Bree's heart leaped as she beamed at Jack.

"If I'm not imposing…" he said.

"Not at all. The aquarium is a lot of fun."

"Then it's decided." He drained his mug.

Bree pushed her chair back and brought her dishes over to the counter. Kay reached for the plate and cup, her eyes twinkling.

"Meet you in the parlor in a few minutes." As Bree hurried away Kay winked at her.

Thirty minutes later Skye, Ella and Bree still waited for Jack to appear. Skye and Ella sat on the loveseat while Bree paced around aimlessly. Barely managing not to bitch about Jack's inconsideration with Ella in the room, she silently fumed. *I can't believe he's blowing his chance to make progress with Ella. He has to stop putting everything else before this child.*

Thuds sounded from the staircase. *Finally.*

Skye and Ella rose from the couch, apparently eager to start the day's adventure. Despite her impatience with him, the sight of Jack brought a sensual tightening in Bree's core. He had changed into fitted black shorts and a chest-hugging, sunny yellow Polo shirt. The body revealing summer clothes emphasized his musculature and had Bree fantasizing about running her hands over taut biceps and abs.

He halted in front of Ella, stooping down to the little girl's eye level. Bree frowned at the sheepish grin he cast his daughter sensing pending disappointment.

"I'm so sorry, baby. But we can't go to the aquarium today. There's trouble…"

The crushed expression on the child's face pierced Bree's heart. "You're *kidding*?" Bree interjected.

"Unfortunately, no," Jack said. "The Michigan plant is down. At the very least, I'll be on the phone all morning."

Kneeling in front of Ella, he gently clasped her hands. "Please understand, honey. I'll work as hard as I can to get this fixed. Maybe we can go to the aquarium tomorrow instead."

"Bree and I can take Ella," Skye volunteered. "If you finish up early, you can join us."

Ella peered through her eyelashes at Jack's face.

Reading her imploring expression, Jack hesitated, "Uh…are you sure it's not imposing?"

"As I mentioned before, I don't consider spending time with Ella an imposition," Bree stated, her tone gruff.

Turning her gaze towards Jack's daughter, she softened her voice, "Is that OK with you, sweetie? Want to have a chick day with us?"

Ella's eyes sparkled as she bobbed her head, yes.

"Then it's a date. Let's go. The sharks are waiting," Skye said.

Bree and Skye each clasped one of Ella's tiny hands and zipped to the front door.

"Bye, sweetheart," Jack said as the trio clattered through the doorway. "Have fun."

Ella sat patiently in the back seat while Bree fastened her safety belt. Taking her place behind the wheel, Bree started the powerful engine and then flicked on the convertible's ragtop switch. The roof glided skyward, accordion folding into the rear compartment.

Skye flung her arms overhead and shouted, "Boys drool; girls rule."

Bree's heart swelled as Ella's soft giggle sounded.

Never too old to enjoy the magical marine life on OBX, a shimmer of familiar anticipation coursed through Bree as she parked the car in the aquarium's nearly empty lot. She purchased tickets at the booth and then she and Skye ushered Ella through the glass doors of the one story building. Dead ahead a mammoth shark skeleton greeted visitors. Its huge mouth gaped open displaying conveyor belt rows of pointy teeth.

"Come on, Ella," Bree said. "Stand inside the jaw. I'll take a picture for your daddy."

A willing model, Ella posed inside the shark's

mouth and then climbed onto a brass alligator for another picture. She even smiled for the camera.

They strolled in front of the glass tanks observing each habitat. A trip to the aquarium with Skye was always extraordinary. The sea creatures sensed her presence and congregated at Skye's position behind the glass.

She greeted each by name: Lemon, Goldy, Bubba...

Bree giggled. "You are making those names up."

Skye smiled slyly. "Maybe I am. And maybe I'm not."

The sea turtle clinic proved a huge hit with Ella who used a stethoscope to examine a plastic baby turtle. Apparently satisfied that the pretend medicine that she injected into her patient had inoculated the creature against diseases of the deep, she sent the turtle down a chute designated as the path into the ocean.

"Let's go see the stingrays," Skye suggested, heading towards the tank.

"You can touch them if you want. But you can only use these two fingers." Bree dipped her index and middle fingers into the water grazing a velvety wing.

The dark shadows skimmed along the bottom of the shallow, circular tank.

Skye whispered, "Myrtle come on over and meet Ella."

A large ray approached and halted in front of Ella. Mesmerized, Ella stroked the fish. "Thank you, Myrtle," Skye said.

The creature appeared to wave its wing as it resumed swimming. Ella was flat-out bewitched.

"Let's wash our hands and head to my favorite

exhibit, The Graveyard of the Atlantic," Bree said.

The area in front of the huge expanse of glass glimmered with reflected cobalt blue light off the water in the tank. Kids pressed their noses against the glass gaping at the leviathans sweeping past a breath away. Bree reveled at the sight of Ella plastered against the tank's wall between two girls about her size—a relief that she could act like any other child.

A huge shark's trajectory veered right at the glass prompting the kids to automatically jump back. Ella's laughter chorusing with the other children was joyful music to Bree.

Jack is going to kick himself when I describe Ella's behavior.

"It makes me sad that Jack isn't here with her," Bree confided to Skye. "How could he let work take precedence over a vacation with his child? These are moments he will never be able to recapture." Bree wagged her head.

"You know me," Skye said softly, "I won't judge. I don't know what it is like to be him. I just know that we were meant to be a part of Ella's life—to really hear her. She has spoken to me since I met her. She'll be talking out loud soon."

Bree grinned and threw her arms around her sister. "You are astonishing, Skye. I love you."

"I love you, too."

On a mission to spoil Ella they followed her meandering path around the gift shop and snapped up items that seemed to put a gleam in the little girl's eyes. Toting a bag stuffed with a plush sea turtle, a floor puzzle, a book on fish and an Outer Banks Aquarium t-shirt, Bree strolled out to the rental car.

"Remember how when we were little, Mom would always make Rice Krispies treats for us when we got home from here?" Bree asked Skye as she drove out of the parking lot.

"Yeah, since that was the only way she could get us to leave," Skye joked.

"Let's stop at Food Lion on the way back and buy the ingredients."

"Sounds good to me." Skye shifted and gazed at Ella in the back seat. "Would you like to help us make them?"

"Yes," Ella responded.

Bree's double take had her reflexively gripping the steering wheel.

"Told you," Skye gleefully muttered under her breath.

****

Bree held Ella's hand traversing the supermarket's parking lot.

"We'll get the cereal. Can you please get the marshmallows?" Bree asked Skye as the automatic door swept open.

In the cereal aisle, Ella scanned the boxes and positioned in front of the Rice Krispies brand. She hovered her hand over a large box of Cocoa Krispies.

"Oh, what a great idea," Bree said. "Let's get a box of regular and chocolate. We better find Skye and tell her we need two bags of marshmallows now."

The pungent stink of marine carcass assaulted Bree's senses as a strident male voice sounded behind her. "Well, hey, Breezy."

Instantly, Bree recognized the speaker as the author of the detested nickname from her high school days.

She turned to face him. "Hello, Randy," Bree said flatly.

Instinctively, Bree clasped Ella's hand tighter. Randy Wyatt hadn't changed much since high school. He still wore his hair in a shag cut, outdated and now thinning at the crown. She had never liked him as a boy.

"I heard you got shot up there in Chitown. But didn't hear you got yourself a little brat, too." He pointed at Ella who leaned heavily against Bree's side.

Edging back a pace Bree opted for polite, empty chitchat. "How's your dad? Still working his fishing boats?" *Absolutely, judging from your reek.*

"Yeah, we still have the boats. Doing pretty good for ourselves." His oily smile revealed a yellow gold incisor.

Inching backward, Ella in tandem, Bree said, "Good to see you. Say hello to your Dad for me."

Turning her back on Randy, Bree ushered Ella out of the aisle and headed toward the candy row.

Provisions for the cereal bars in hand, Bree led the dash to the express lane.

Leaving the parking lot, Bree spied Randy standing outside the door and gawking at her car.

Bree gave a head tilt towards the market. "That guy gives me the creeps," she whispered to Skye.

"Really?" Skye swiveled her head and gazed out the window. "Randy Wyatt? He always impressed me as pathetic. Smells to high heaven."

****

Bree found Kay in the kitchen when she, Ella and Skye returned home. Two large pots of melting butter simmered on the stove.

"The butter's almost ready." Kay hummed as she swirled a spatula in the pot.

No surprise. Her mother usually knew what Bree or her sisters intended to do before they did.

"How was the aquarium?" Kay asked as she placed one of the pots on a divot on the wooden table.

"A lot of fun." Bree nabbed a marshmallow as Skye emptied a bag into the pot.

Bree pilfered another marshmallow before it could melt and handed it to Ella who stuffed the whole candy into her mouth.

Standing next to Kay at the stove, Bree looked on while Skye and Ella added the cereal to the pot.

"I wonder if Jack appreciates how he missed out today. Ma, she actually said a word," Bree related, speaking softly.

"Oh that's marvelous!"

"I know. And he wasn't there. Maybe you spoiled us, but I always knew that we were your number one priority."

"A child is a gift from God. Nothing or no one is more important to me and your father than you girls."

"Where is Jack?"

"I haven't seen him all day. Must be in his room."

Bree lingered a minute watching Jack's daughter smile and giggle with Skye.

"I'll be right back."

Chapter 8

Pausing outside Jack's room, Bree raised her arm, poised to rap on the door. His deep bass voice boomed from within; the low to high tones ranging from engine idle rumble to thunder on Mount Olympus. Problems with the Michigan plant apparently had yet to be resolved.

Her inherent courtesy had her reluctant to confront him over her dim view of his parenting skills while he obviously was doing his job. She hated when someone interrupted her work and typically respected others accordingly.

Still. Ella is more important.

Before she could hesitate further, Bree knocked sharply three times, shaking the heavy wooden door on its hinges. She could hear stirring within and then he said clearly, "Hold on."

The door swung open revealing Jack wearing creased black shorts, a grim expression and a cell phone that he shoulder-shrugged up to his ear. "I'm busy," he said.

She read his tone as dismissive and her irritation blossomed into anger. "I *need* to speak with you. May I come in?"

Jack's brow furrowed and he wagged his head, no. "I'll come find you when I'm off the phone?"

No longer concerned about rudeness, she

shouldered past him into the room, and spun around squaring off with Jack. "I need to talk to you *now*."

Narrowing his eyes, he said into the phone, "I'll have to call you back." And then he lowered the phone from his ear, glanced at the screen, tapped disconnect and pocketed the device.

"This better be important." He applied just enough emphasis to each word to stoke Bree's temper.

"Certainly more important than money," she retorted.

His eyes darkened ominously. "Is that what you think I'm about? Money is everything?"

Standing her ground, she shot back, "Apparently— since work undoubtedly comes before everything with you."

"Is that so?" He planted his brawny body directly in front of Bree. "And the *doctor* doesn't approve of my supposed money grubbing, huh? Seems to me I shelled out *plenty* to child shrinks just like you who happily pocketed exorbitant fees and *buzz*—cut off each session at sixty minutes like clockwork. Next."

"Now wait just a minute…"

"I'm not just providing for my daughter. I have to worry about the hundreds of employees in that Michigan plant who are working for me to provide for *their* families. I take that responsibility seriously or I'd sleep less at night than I already do. You couldn't possibly understand…" he trailed off.

Her chest heaved and she gaped up at him defiant, fighting for composure. "What I *understand* is that you have fooled yourself into believing that altruism forgives your neglect of your daughter."

Ignoring his clenched jaw and refusing to give him

an opening to retaliate, she forged on. "She's obviously traumatized. She needs your undivided attention. Such a little thing, spending time with a child. She hardly knows Skye or me. Yet she's responding—improving."

"How the hell do you know?" he spat out. "You have no idea—"

"She spoke today," Bree interjected.

As if she pierced his ballooning anger with a pin, the storm clouds in his eyes evaporated. "She *did*? What did she say?"

Jack's soft eyes exuded wonderstruck hope. His gray eyes glassy, she detected tears welling.

Bree's heart somersaulted and the mad seeped out of her. "Yes. She said, yes."

He bowed his head. "My God that's unbelievable," he whispered.

Raising his head, he gazed deeply into Bree's eyes. "Thank you for helping her...for telling me..."

In the next instant, his powerful arms encircled her and Bree was swept up off the ground and spun a full circle. Giddy, she arched her back, her eyes on the ceiling enjoying the dizzying sensations. This broody man certainly jumbled her emotions. One minute she wanted to pummel his chest with her fists and the next she melted against the hard planes of him giving in to the rush of desire that he stirred in her. She wanted to fuse her body to his, press ever tighter heartbeat-to-heartbeat.

She laced her arms around Jack's neck as he stood in place. Still holding her aloft at eye level, his parted lips were a breath away from hers. He smelled like the Inn's French milled soap and something musky, clean—his own tantalizing scent. Bree anticipated the kiss, closing her eyes and tilting her head to meet his full lips with hers. His clasp around her waist tightened as he deepened the kiss and her breasts pressed against his chest. Heat enveloped her stoking her fervent answer. She parted her lips and thrilled as their tongues intertwined.

He gently ended the kiss, and Bree gazed at his face, enraptured. Jack's eyes were closed, giving her no hint about what he was feeling in that moment. She had never been kissed like that; spun beyond gravity and spellbound.

When he opened his eyes and trained his gaze on Bree's face, his dazed expression thrilled her to the core. His clasp loosened and he guided her gradual, sensual slide down to the floor. The friction between their bodies scintillated her.

Gazing up at him, she grinned. "You're welcome."

****

The woman bewitched Jack and knocked him off-center. Her appeal to him defied logic. She had burst into his room, a know-it-all firebrand—a member of a profession that had offered nothing but false hope ever since Gabriella shut down communication. He didn't kiss women like those—no less want more. Much more.

"How did you do that?" he asked, referring to the unexpected miracle of spurring Gabriella to speak.

Her sea green eyes sparkled. "I was going to ask you the same thing," she teased.

He chuckled. "I meant how did you break through with Gabriella?"

Bree knit her brow. "Oh. Um...do you want to pretend that this," she tapped her index finger on her lips, "never happened?"

Jack focused on her lips, his gaze lingering, her peppermint sweet taste still on his tongue. He had no intention of pretending anything with Bree. But she scrambled his brain with her powerful effect on him and his daughter. Jack Tremonti, computer whiz and founder of the most successful tech company on the planet, could not abide jumbled thoughts.

"Before I analyze why I kissed you, I think I'd like to understand what you've done with my daughter," he said carefully.

She narrowed her eyes to slits. "*Analyze?*"

Averting his gaze, she stared at the carpet instead. He envisioned sparks flying out of her pupils sufficient to set the room on fire.

"Bree, I'm sorry. You have me confused. I'm not used to that."

"Let me help *you* analyze." The glance she cast him was razor sharp—the queen of psychiatric analysis cutting the tech nerd down to size. "I suppose you kissed me out of gratitude."

"No, I…"

She waved off further comment. "And if that is the case, your gesture was misplaced. I didn't do anything to Ella other than provide attention and warm company—something *you* haven't done since you got here, by the way. Skye undoubtedly worked her magic on Ella and she deserves the credit.

"I guess you'll want to go kiss Skye now?" she concluded, her tone sarcastic.

Jack hooted a laugh. He couldn't help it, despite his sure knowledge that it would piss her off more. He kind of enjoyed her spitfire mode. Draping his arms over her shoulders he added another nail to his coffin. "She looks exactly like you. I'm sure I'll enjoy kissing her just as much."

She squirmed like a fish dragged onto a boat deck and tensed as he corralled her within his embrace. He kissed her squarely on the lips again. "I'm not toying with you, Bree. I appreciate with my whole heart that you and your family are helping my little girl. But my kissing you has nothing to do with that."

Apparently appeased, she relaxed in his arms. "All right. Do you want me to tell you about Ella's morning?"

"Sure. Come sit down." He pointed to the deck chairs out on the balcony as his cell phone blared and erupted in vibrations in his pocket.

He didn't answer the call garnering a smile from Bree. "I'm still up to my ass in alligators with the Michigan plant. I'll have to get back to work soon."

"This won't take long," she said heading out through the sliding door.

Jack sat opposite her leaning his elbows on his knees. The breeze played through her hair. She tamed the flying auburn wisps, tucking them behind her ears. Sunlight kissed, her creamy complexion glowed angelic. The waves pounded a rhythmic melody on the shore. Bree smiled and Jack relished the prospect of hearing good news about his beloved child from this beautiful woman who magically had become extremely important to him.

"Skye has heard Ella speaking all along," Bree stated as if the illogical statement were fact.

"Whoa, what?"

She flicked her eyes skyward. "Skye is... highly intuitive. Anyway, we spent time at every habitat at the aquarium," she continued rapidly. "Ella particularly loved the sea turtle clinic. She loved everything actually."

"You call her Ella. Does she like that?"

"Seems to. Again, Skye started using the nickname and since she seemed so connected to Gabriella, we all followed suit."

He nodded and considered using the nickname himself, but immediately rejected the idea. To him, she'd always be Gabriella.

"On the way back, Skye asked Ella if she wanted to help make marshmallow Rice Krispies treats and Ella responded, yes. Clearly. I was driving and I almost crashed the car." She gave him a lopsided grin.

He clasped her hands in his. "Thank you, God. Do you think she'll continue to talk?"

The idea that this one syllable that he'd missed hearing her utter was a one-time thing made Jack shudder.

"I do," she said sunnily. "But you have to get involved, Jack, if you want her to talk to you."

"I will." He stood gently towing Bree to her feet. "I'm going to deal with this problem in Michigan as fast as I can and then spend time with her for the rest of the day. Are you going to eat dinner here this evening?"

"I am."

"Good. Let me see you to the door."

Jack turned the knob and Bree slipped past him through the threshold. She faced him in the hallway. "See you later."

"I hope so." Pensive, he closed the door and leaned against it. Far too objective to give credence to supernatural forces, Jack tried to find a logical explanation for his and Gabriella's behavior since they had arrived here.

Stymied, he searched out the brochure that Mike had given him and reread *The Legend of the Three Butterflies.*

Chapter 9

His stomach rolled as the waves crashed against his ship. A percussion of cannon fire chilled him to the bone. The merchant sloop pitched as the Queen Anne's Revenge bumped into its side and Teach's crew boarded. He had heard tales of Blackbeard's leniency and prayed it was true. He stumbled along the rail trying to reach his wife and babies. He felt the sword enter his back as he cried out his wife's name. My love, I am so sorry. Sarah. Maeve. Breeze. Gabriella. The names echoed in the wind. He watched as three red butterflies took flight off the bow of the ship and he smiled.

Jack bolted awake. Sweat dripped off his forehead. His hands shook as he rubbed his hands across his face. For an instant, his surroundings were foreign to him. He breathed a deep sigh of relief as he recognized his room at the Inn. Still affected by the strange nightmare, he bolted out of bed and raced to the door that separated his room from his daughter. Gabriella lay sound asleep buried beneath the covers. Her thin arm clutched a stuffed dolphin close to her cheek. Jack tucked a strand of silken hair behind her ear, kissed the top of her head and then tiptoed back to his room. Sitting heavily on the edge of the bed he lit the lamp. The trifold pamphlet he had reread yesterday on the end table caught his eye— the obvious source of the haunting dream. Even awake, the nightmare's agony of loss stayed with him. He drew back the drapes and slid open the sliding glass door, stepping out on the balcony. Creamy moonlight shimmered on the waves. The wind off the surf ruffled his hair. *Bree is right. Nothing is more important than Gabriella.*

Jack ducked inside the room, grabbed his laptop off the desk, perched on the end of his bed and sent out emails to his top people. For twenty-four hours, he would not be available by phone or email—no matter what. Happy with his decision, he shut down the computer and stowed it in his briefcase. He strolled out again onto the balcony. The thundering waves blotted out any other sounds as he settled into the wicker chair to watch the sunrise, and think about how he might spend the day with his daughter.

He must have dozed. Seagull squawks woke him. A toilet flushed prompting him to hurry back into his room.

Gabriella emerged from the bathroom.

"Good morning, sweetheart."

Although she didn't return the greeting, she tightened her arms around him when he hugged her, encouraging Jack.

"I'm starving. Let's go get some breakfast. As usual, something smells good." Clasping her hand, he led her out the door, leaving his phone behind.

Bright sunshine streamed through sparkling kitchen windows painting rainbows on the white tile floor. A light breeze through the screens ruffled the lacy curtains adding to the homey cheer.

"Don't get up," Jack said as Mike made to rise from his seat at the table. "I can get my own coffee."

Mike jumped up anyway. "I'll just whip up some chocolate milk for the princess," he said winking at Gabriella, who beamed him a smile.

Jack's heart melted at her reaction to the loving care of their host.

Kay strode into the room carrying a vase shaped like an open-mouthed fish filled with sunflowers. She set the arrangement in the middle of Jack's table. Bree and Skye trailed Kay carrying similar vases.

"Where do you want these?" Skye asked.

"On the counter would be perfect," Kay said. "Thank you, girls."

Mike pecked a kiss on Kay's cheek. "The flowers are lovely. I wondered where you rushed off to this morning after your walk."

"Harris Teeter's fresh flower supply arrives early. I had my heart set on sunflowers and they disappear fast." She bustled around the kitchen checking the chafing dishes.

Jack filled two plates and sat next to Gabriella. He forked up a bite of savory food and then said, "I know I sound like a broken record Kay, but this casserole is delicious."

"Thanks. I never tire of hearing that you like my cooking." Kay took a seat at the head of the table setting down a cup of tea at her place.

Gabriella wolfed down the meal.

"Looks like my girl likes your cooking, too," Jack quipped.

"What are you two up to today?" Kay eyed him over the rim of her mug.

"Nothing definite. I just want to devote the day to my girl." He rubbed Gabriella's back and was rewarded with a cheese-smeared, toothy grin. "Any suggestions?"

"There are so many wonderful things to do here. What are you up for?"

"Sightseeing? Sand dune climbing? Paddle board lessons? Jet skiing? Deep sea fishing?" Skye rattled off.

"Or maybe you two would just enjoy spending the day walking and talking along miles of beaches." Bree gazed at him pointedly and smiled.

"Great idea." He winked at her. *I paid attention, lady.* "How about we build sand castles and go seashell hunting? What do you think, sweetheart?"

"That's the perfect way to spend this day, Ella," Skye said. "I wish I could join you, but a seagull is badgering me to paint his portrait."

"And I have to spend the day doing chores," Bree said.

Jack doubted Bree's claim and almost called her out. But he wanted to reconnect with his daughter even more than he wanted to connect with Bree. That said a lot.

"I'll pack a little lunch for you." Kay popped up from the table. She opened the pantry door and lifted a small cooler up from the floor.

"Come on, Ella. I'll give you my favorite sand shovels and pails. Oh—and a net bag for all the shells you'll find," Skye said, extending her hand.

Ella linked hands with Skye beaming her a high wattage smile. The child's giggles as they left the room filled Jack with well-being. But he remained insecure about whether he was on the right track today.

"She seems to be enjoying everyone here, except... Maybe I should ask you and Skye to come with us, Bree. I'm not sure Gabriella will enjoy being alone with me." Jack stared into his cup of coffee.

"Don't be like that," Bree said softly. "It's going to take a little time. Or maybe it's going to take a long time. But you have to start somewhere and most importantly without any distractions. Some of my happiest memories growing up were days spent alone with my dad."

Mike strode behind Bree's chair and brushed a soft kiss on the top of her head. "Remember our day at Busch Gardens? How you dragged your old man on every roller coaster in the park?"

"Whoa, wait one minute! It was the other way around. I hate roller coasters. But we had a blast. That's what I mean, Jack. A little girl will never forget the time her father spends with her. I know I never will.

"If you make her your number one priority, she'll never forget it. Trust me. Through the years she won't remember how much you spent on her or the luxuries you provided. She'll hold in her heart the walks and the talks and the feeling of being number one."

Flip flop slaps echoed as Ella and Skye appeared, the latter toting a net bag filled with sand toys.

Kay closed the lid on the cooler and placed it by the door. Mike went to the cupboard and loaded his arms with sunscreen and towels.

Accepting the provisions from his hosts, Jack said, "Thanks. You guys think of everything."

"Years and years of practice taking little princesses to the beach," Mike said on a laugh.

"I left my phone upstairs. I'll be right back, Gabriella," Jack said.

"Can't you forget about your phone for one day?" Came Bree's voice as he bounded up the first three stairs toward the second floor.

He spun around, descended and backtracked towards her. "I listened to you last night. Honestly. I haven't thought of anything else. I shouldn't have let business interfere with my vacation with her. I want the phone with me for emergencies and for pictures. I'm officially off for the day."

His heart swelled as a radiant smile bloomed on Bree's lovely face. This woman really cared about his daughter and he was starting to care very much for this woman. He stepped close and smiled at her, lost in the sea green depths of her eyes. "I promise today will be all about Gabriella. Tell you the truth, I'm nervous."

"Don't be. Just be yourself. That's what she needs now. Just to be with you and know she's safe."

"Thank you." He dipped his head and tenderly kissed her lips.

"My pleasure. Go have fun."

****

Following Mike's directions, Jack drove the rental car to Pea Island. The Laytons had deemed the beach here perfect for their father daughter day. The view from the Bonner Bridge was breathtaking. Boats dotted the aquamarine waters and the sun was bright in the powder blue sky. In the rearview mirror, Jack watched Gabriella's dividing her attention between the panoramas on the left and right.

"Isn't this beautiful scenery?" he said.

Her reflection in the mirror looked directly into his eyes as she gifted him with a head nod, yes. Thrilled about even the slightest response, he rambled, "Look at those boats. Skye sure is lucky living here. We'll have to come back again sometime. Does that sound like a good idea?"

Another head nod enhanced his good mood.

Jack parked in the lot at the visitor's center. Gabriella stood silently by his side as he unloaded the trunk.

"Damn it! I left the cooler at the Inn."

He observed her shuddering and instantly regretted the outburst. "I'm sorry. I didn't mean to scare you. We'll find a place to eat lunch after we build the biggest sand castle that Pea Island has ever seen."

Taking hold of her hand, he waited for traffic to clear, crossed the road and then climbed the sandy path over the dunes towards the ocean.

The sun sparkled diamond glints on the rippled surface of the water. The beach was deserted. Jack wafted two beach towels in turn. The brightly colored material fluttered outward before he tamed their flight and spread them on the sand anchored at the corners by their gear.

Jack tugged his t-shirt off over his head and plopped it on one of the beach towels.

"Let's go for a walk first and look for shells," he said. Jack stooped down to help her take off her sandals, happy as she leaned her little body against his shoulder for balance.

They walked hand in hand at the water's edge. Around and far ahead of him, the sand appeared smooth—almost raked—without a single shell in sight. The waves lapped gently over his bare feet, cooling and refreshing.

"You know I love you, Gabriella, don't you?"

She nodded in response.

"Maybe you think it's my fault that Mommy died.

I'm so very sorry, honey. I should have picked you up from class instead of Mommy. I wish with all my heart that we had that day back to live over. But we don't and we have to go on without her. You know Mommy wouldn't want you to be unhappy."

Jack held her hand tighter as she strained to tug free of his grasp. "Please, sweetheart. Talk to me."

Gabriella yanked her hand away and fled down the beach.

Crestfallen, he gave chase, calling her name repeatedly. She halted twenty feet ahead of him. He caught up and knelt in the sand in front of her. His heart breaking, he gently wiped the tears from her eyes with his thumbs.

"I'm sorry," he said again. He'd apologize forever if he could break through. "I don't want to ruin our day together. I just want you to know that I love you with all my heart and that I'm here for you when and if you want to talk to me about anything."

He hugged her—a tiny little block of wood. He had to keep chipping away.

"Can I have a do over?" He tilted her chin up. "Please look at me."

She obeyed casting him a dull gaze. "Can we start all over?"

No response.

"Let's build a sand castle like I promised." He traipsed back down the beach, hoping she'd follow. Scooping up a red pail off the beach towel, he strode into the shallows, filled the bucket to the brim and left it atop the slope of the wet sand apron at the shore's edge. Retracing his steps back toward the beach towels, he picked up a shovel, sloshed back through shifting sand to where he had left the pail and dug damp sand into a heap. Observing her approach out of the corner of his eye, he plopped down on the ground next to the mound and began shaping the pile of sand into the castle's foundation. The more he patted, the more the sand slipped off the mound. "Maybe a little more water would help. Sweetheart, can you pour some water in the hole?"

She hoisted the pail off the ground, both hands clutching the handle, but it proved too heavy and she dropped it. Water splashed directly into his face. He squinted up at her, droplets dripping off his nose. Her lip quivered.

Jack shook his head rapidly back and forth spraying her with water as he burst out laughing. She giggled. He jumped up, lifted her into his arms in a fireman's carry and bolted into the sea. He held her tight as a swell rolled by and then lowered her to stand next to him on the ocean floor.

Tethered by tight handclasps, Jack and his daughter laughed and jumped the waves. It was going to take time, but in his heart he knew they would be all right.

Chapter 10

Jack twisted the shower valve shut with a rapid flick of his wrist, straining to identify the faint sound that he had heard. His mouth hung open as the sweet sound registered. Gabriella was humming her bedtime song—the song he had sung to her every night since she was an infant. As a toddler she had absolutely refused to go to sleep before he had provided a rendition. No matter where he was in the world he had used his technology to sing her to sleep.

She loved the bass part and even before she had learned to talk she chorused "bah dah dah" along with him. Until she had shut off communication and left him a helpless soloist every bedtime since.

He interpreted the nostalgic muffled sounds emanating from her room as an invitation. Jack hustled out of the shower, briskly dried off with a towel and slipped into fresh clothes. Flinging open the two rooms' connecting door which he had hung ajar before showering, he sang the lyrics, full voiced and at top volume. Thoroughly happy with his silliness he grinned into her shining eyes.

When she sang the bass riff with him, albeit very softly, his heart burst with glee. This complicated, monumental, prayed-for occurrence now seemed such a simple thing to Jack as his little girl rolled onto her side and snuggled deeper into the bedcovers when he finished singing. At her bedside in three strides, Jack kissed her baby soft cheek and whispered, as he had thousands of times, "Good night, sweetheart."

"Good night, Daddy," came the longed for, prayed for, miracle response.

Tears stung his eyes and he choked back a sob. "I'm going downstairs to spend some time with Bree if she's around," he said, barely managing to keep his voice steady and matter of fact in the wake of this, please God, permanent breakthrough. "Call me on my cell phone from the phone on your bed table if you need me?"

"Uh huh," she agreed, her eyes already closed.

He scarcely believed that they had actually engaged in a dialogue.

Jack left her room when she fell asleep, happiness circulating inside him like a life-saving transfusion. This was too huge to keep to himself; he had to share the news, describe this euphoric feeling to someone who might understand. As he had informed Gabriella, he chose Bree.

Descending the back stairway leading to the kitchen, Jack halted on the second from the bottom step listening to Bree hum "Goodnight Sweetheart, Goodnight."

He took the last two steps down in one leap and emerged into the kitchen grinning. "You heard?"

Bree stopped humming and raised her head towards him, her hands immersed in sudsy water at the sink. Her eyes crinkled at the corners as she smiled. "I passed your room on the way downstairs. It was hard to miss your singing." She chuckled. "I loved that song in *Three Men and A Baby*."

Jack came up behind her and circled his arms around her waist. She leaned back against him and her satiny crown tucked under his chin. He breathed in her springtime scent, happy just to hold her near in the quiet kitchen while his little girl slept soundly above him. "Did you hear her sing with me, Bree?" he asked, his mouth close to her petal soft ear lobe.

She shifted within his arms, made a slight turn and arched her neck to look over her shoulder. Gazing up at him, her eyes widened. "I didn't, no. But that's wonderful! Did she..."

He silenced her with a penetrating kiss, deeper, increasingly deeper as if he poured his entire heart into the intimacy. She moaned softly in the back of her throat—a sexy vibration against his devouring lips. Jack gently grasped her shoulders and pirouetted her to face him. He drew her forward to clasp her close to his heart. She yelped and her body jerked beneath his hands.

"What?" Aghast that he had unwittingly hurt her, he fanned his fingers and whipped his hands off of her shoulders.

Jack frowned as Bree cupped her right shoulder with her left hand, spraying soapsuds, and gently massaged it in circles—pain evident in the squint of her lovely green eyes.

"I'm sorry. I didn't mean to be rough. Are you all right?"

She gave him a thin smile and his stomach sank a little lower because he had evidently caused her pain when he *only* meant to give her pleasure.

Taking much longer to recover from the apparently aggressive squeeze than he would have liked, her fragility confused him. "Honest, I didn't realize I was so rough. Do you want to sit down?"

Bree dropped her left hand to her side and rolled her shoulders several times. "No, I'm good now. You weren't rough at all." She touched his arm softly. And then a mischievous glint sparked in her eyes.

In the next instant, Bree's slender arms encircled his neck and her soft breasts pressed against his ribcage—exactly his originally intended maneuver. She arched her neck and gazed up at him smiling.

Her russet hair fell away from her face in a riot of coppery tendrils down her back. She wore no makeup on her porcelain skin—just a touch of coral color on her lips and maybe a few strokes of black mascara feathered on long eyelashes. Bree's style was so unlike Sophia's vanity and full-makeup-before-facing-the-world mentality. There wasn't a trace of deception or bitchiness in the soulful depths of her eyes—another stark contrast to Sophia. *Just sweetness, kindness, honesty, intelligence and sexiness. God, yes, sexiness.*

Careful not to hurt her this time, Jack placed one hand on her lower back to draw her closer to him and then he threaded his hand up through the soft hair at the nape of her neck. Cupping the back of her head, he dove right back into the singular, heady pleasure of kissing Bree Layton. In addition to inspiring him to be a more sensitive father, this woman went beyond the impossible for Jack on one other count. When kissing her, not one single thought fired in his overactive brain. She blotted out everything but the need for more…

****

Mindless with desire, Bree was tempted to rip off Jack's shirt and then her own blouse in rapid succession, right there in the middle of the kitchen. She melted into his kiss surrendering to every delicious sensation—the varying pressure of his lips on hers and the fiery tangling of their tongues. She absolutely *had* to make love with Jack.

But not now. Not here.

She effected a cool-down by ending the kiss and nestling her head on his broad shoulder.

Jack muttered, "Wow."

Her heart beat wildly and every over-stimulated nerve ending shimmied inside her. No one had *ever* kissed her like that. The dawning knowledge had her musing about how mind blowing full union might be with him. She hoped that she'd find out.

"I didn't hurt you again, did I?" His breath spread warmth on the top of her head.

"Uh uh." She laid her hand on his chest thrilling at the solid heat of his body, his thudding heartbeat beneath her palm. "It's a recent injury. You couldn't have known."

Bree closed her eyes, deeply content at the soft pressure of his lips kissing her crown. "Want to tell me about it?"

"Get a *room*." Summer's teasing voice sounded to Bree's right.

Jack released Bree from his embrace and he took a step backward. Knitting her brow, her lips pursed in amusement, Bree faced her sister.

Summer grinned at Bree, her eyes dancing. "Good thing Daddy didn't walk in here instead of me." She edged past Jack and Bree who stood woodenly apart in front of the sink.

Yanking on the refrigerator handle, Summer swung

open the door, bent slightly at the waist and peered inside. A waft of cool air fanned Bree's overheated face. She wasn't the least embarrassed at being caught in a clinch with Jack—by Summer instead of her father.

"I'm stealing these and packing it for the drive to Norfolk Airport." Summer held up a couple Tupperware containers full of leftovers.

"You have to leave?"

"Yeah, tomorrow. Mom doesn't need me; and duty calls." Toting the food containers, she headed toward the stairs. "I'll be awake for a while in our room if you want to talk later, Bree. In the mean time, I'll leave you two to…"

Bree hooted a laugh as Summer left the room. She faced Jack. His soft gray-blue eyes radiated mirth and a smile played at the corners of his lips. His obvious great mood had transformed his features from darkly handsome to charm the pants off of you gorgeous. Remembering that she still knew little about Jack, she chose to exercise caution.

"Want to walk on the beach for a while?" she said. "There's a full moon and plenty of light."

"Sure." He held out his hand.

Bree nabbed a back door key from the basket on the counter, pocketed it and then linked her hand in Jack's.

Outside the sea breeze stirred the humid air and the rush of the ocean filled her ears. Balancing with one hand atop the deck's newel post, she kicked off her sandals. Jack removed his shoes and set them next to hers. She bounded down the steps, Jack at her side. Keeping pace, her hand clasped lightly in his, they set off down the beach.

"Tell me everything about Ella's progress."

"I heard her humming. She sang with me. Then she said good night. And then she answered me when I told her I was leaving the room. To find you…"

Bree stopped short and threw her arms around him, exuberant at the good news about Ella and elated that he had purposefully sought her out to share his happiness. She peered up at his shadowed face. "I'm so happy for you, Jack. So happy for Ella."

He kissed her forehead and then said, "Do you think it's real? Will it last?"

She clasped his hand again and resumed strolling. "Her behavior is definitely real. It signifies a genuine need for reconnection with you. Though without knowing what caused her to shut down in the first place, I can't predict with certainty if this is temporary or not."

"Shit. I was hoping you'd say that the nightmare is over. I don't know what I'll do if she stops talking again."

"Stay the course for the rest of your week here. See where it goes." She bumped her shoulder against his in solidarity. "Ouch! Damn, I keep forgetting."

"What's wrong with your arm?"

"My shoulder. A gunshot wound three months ago."

"You were *shot*? How the hell did that happen? Don't tell me a crazy patient…"

"No. I'm not treating any gun-toting children." She huffed a laugh. "I was doing a favor for an old friend and you could say it backfired."

"What kind of a favor involves guns?"

Bree halted and gazed at the water. The moon

reflected an undulating ribbon of butter colored light atop the waves. "I took a Criminal Psychology course in college and met Vinnie in class. We dated for a while when we were sophomores. Anyway, Vinnie's an FBI agent now. He had a case in Chicago and he asked me to do some unofficial consulting for him. Psychological profiling for a homicide suspect."

In motion again back towards the Inn, Jack in tow, Bree added, "I went with him when he interviewed a suspect at her home, and she shot me. One minute I was sitting across the table from her and the next I was laid out on the floor and it seemed like my shoulder was on fire."

"Good God. Your friend dragged you into something like that? Did he get shot, too?"

"Oh no. He didn't drag me. I volunteered. The profile I compiled pointed toward this suspect, but nobody believed that the murderer was a woman. I hounded him to let me go with him to question her. I wanted to see if I was right or not. He literally saved my life during the incident."

"I wouldn't have let you come."

Bree huffed a laugh. "Yes, you would have. I can be very stubborn. I was right, after all."

"Maybe. But I still wouldn't have exposed you to danger like that."

"Well. It's all behind me now," she said. "Come on. I'll race you to the deck. Loser buys *me* dinner tomorrow night."

"Pretty confident, aren't you?" he joked.

She tore off laughing. Jack's heavy footfalls pounded the earth behind her and then he streaked past Bree. His rapid clip launched a sandstorm in his wake.

Sprinting, Bree strained to catch up with him. He braked abruptly and pivoted in his tracks. On the fly she crashed into his chest.

Her lungs afire from exertion, she leaned against him.

"I'll gladly buy you dinner tomorrow," he said folding her in his arms. "How about a good night kiss before we go inside?"

Chapter 11

Bree lifted her head, turned over her pillow for the tenth time, sank her head back down and willed her brain to stop whirling. How could a simple goodnight kiss change everything? When Jack had first teased her with a brush of his lips against hers, one of a kind electrical zingers at his touch had coursed through her. *But...* When he cupped her face in his hands and *really* kissed her, high voltage zapped Bree, fusing her with him, consumed. Breathless, the sensations had spiraled as if the sheer force of attraction would lift them both off the ground. When he withdrew his lips she had clung to him shaking. If she had let go, she might have pooled into a puddle at his feet.

Jack had murmured, "Wow," as he nodded his head over her crown.

Had even a percentage of similar reactions swamped him? Had fireworks exploded behind his closed eyelids, too? Bree had only seen a kiss like that in the movies. It was the kind of kiss that made the cartoon skunk's heart beat out of his chest.

Raising her head again, she flipped her pillow over and pounded it into shape.

"What did that pillow ever do to you?" Summer's raspy voice sounded.

"I'm sorry," Bree whispered. "I didn't mean to wake you."

"When one of us can't sleep, you know the three of us can't sleep," Skye murmured as she rolled over and switched on the lamp on the end table between Bree's bed and hers. Its soft pink light cast a rosy glow on the walls.

"What's up? Are you OK?" Skye scooted up, leaned against the wicker headboard and dragged the pink striped sheet up to her shoulders.

Summer covered her face with her pillow. "Must be a boy," she mumbled.

Skye hooted a laugh. "It's always a boy."

Bree smiled as she flung off the sheet and swung her legs over the side of her bed. "How many nights have we sat up in these beds and talked about boys? I guess some things never change."

Apparently giving up on sleep, Summer tossed her pillow to the foot of her bed. "Except now the boys have become sexy, virile hunks." She winked at Skye. "If we're talking about Jack, that is."

Facing Bree, she arched her eyebrows, a smile teasing the corners of her mouth. "Are we talking about Jack?"

Restless and agitated, Bree didn't know how to broach the topic of "Jack" quite yet. She rose off the bed. "Really I'm sorry to wake you both up. It's almost sunrise. I'm going to throw on my bathing suit and walk on the beach. Go back to sleep. I'll see you both later."

Surprised that her sisters kept mum, Bree rummaged in her suitcase on the luggage rack in front of her bed, nabbed a black one-piece bathing suit and scooted into the bathroom, closing the door behind her.

When she emerged after dressing and brushing her

teeth, Bree wasn't surprised to find her sisters already clad in bathing suits and sitting on the edge of their beds. *When one of us can't sleep, so go the three of us.*

"I have to head back to New York this morning," Summer said as she rushed ahead of Skye to take her turn in the bathroom. "I don't know when I'll see you guys again so I don't want to waste a minute of sister time by sleeping."

Skye used the bathroom last and then the trio scrambled down the back staircase.

Outside, the magnificent sunrise had them pulling up short at the top of the stairs that led to the beach. Bree sighed appreciatively at the spectacle, which never failed to fill her with gratitude for God's ever changing palette of colors in the sky—today, streaks of vivid crimson and fuchsia. The sun hadn't yet breached the horizon. It seemed the low clouds were afire with its pending arrival.

"Did you ever wish you could stop time?" Skye's soft voice floated on the breeze. Bree and Summer nodded, yes.

"If I could, I would stop time right this instant while we're standing here together. We used to be inseparable. I really miss you both when you're not here."

The spontaneous group hug tangled the three of them together laughing.

"Come on," Bree said as she kicked off her sandals and started down the stairs.

Summer and Skye flanking her, Bree strolled to the water's edge and set off down the beach sloshing through the shallows. Outgoing waves sucked at the sand beneath Bree's toes and the frigid seawater lapping against her ankles and shins chilled her. Exhilarated, there was nowhere on earth she'd rather be in that moment.

"I don't want to go back today. I wish I could stay forever," Summer declared.

"You read my mind," Bree said.

Summer picked up a small shell, rubbed it between her fingers and then tossed it into the trough of an onrushing wave. "I've been thinking a lot lately about making a change. I don't think the big city," she said miming air quotes, "lives up to the hype anymore."

Bree smiled at the childhood reference to what the triplets called New York. Every year their dad packed the family into the car and made the nine-hour drive to what the girls had called the Big City. They stayed overnight in a hotel, went to the Rockette's Christmas performance at Radio City Music Hall and gaped at the huge decorated tree in Rockefeller Center. Bree, Skye and Summer were amazed by the skyscrapers, the blazing lights, more cars than they could count and the scents of exotic food. The noisiness of New York City left a lasting impression on Bree and her sisters. Car horns blared, brakes screeched and people yelled at each other whether in friendship or anger.

"Remember how huge and noisy everything seemed?" Skye said.

"I remember that out of all of us you were the most frightened by the place." Bree swept her arm around Skye's shoulder and gave it a squeeze. "You were the happiest to cross the Bay Bridge-Tunnel on the way back. You knew you were getting close to home.

"You belong here, Skye," Bree concluded. "I think Summer and I are still trying to figure out where we belong."

"Bree's right. As soon as I drive over the Wright Bridge and hit the mainland on the way to the airport, I'm already thinking about the next time that I can come back."

"When do you think that will be, Summer?" Skye asked.

"I don't know. I'll definitely be here for July 4th but I don't think I will be able to get away from work before then."

I wonder if Jack is up yet. I can't wait to be with him again.

Bree placed her hand over her midriff at the fluttering in her stomach at the prospect of seeing Jack. She lagged behind her sisters, lost in reverie.

"Earth to Bree," Summer teased.

"What?" Bree blinked at her sister. "I'm sorry. I guess I wasn't listening."

"Obviously." Skye laughed. "I asked you when you're coming back after this visit."

"Oh…" she stammered. "I really haven't given it much thought."

"OK, spill it," Summer demanded.

"Spill what?"

"Your head has been in the clouds this whole time. What's that about? What made you beat your pillow up all night?"

Bree shrugged her shoulders. "Can't keep a thing from you two that's for sure. Well… Do you think a single kiss can be monumental? I mean, life changing?"

"I assume Jack kissed you, right?" Skye slid her sunglasses up over the top of her head.

"Oh yeah. I walked in on them in the kitchen last

night." Fanning her face and grinning, Summer sat down and patted a spot on the sand next to her. "Sit here, Bree. Tell us about it and don't leave out a single detail."

Bree plopped down on the soft sand next to Summer. Skye followed suit and the threesome bumped shoulders as they stretched their legs out in front of them, the warm granules of sand coating the backs of their legs.

Intense love for her siblings swelled inside Bree. "I love you both so much. I don't know what I would ever do without you."

Bree paused, musing about how to express her feelings. "This may sound crazy because honestly I feel a little crazy. But when Jack kissed me I felt...transformed. Really different in a physical sense as if my entire body changed in that moment. Kind of like—you know—when we were kids. I thought the sensation would pass after I slept and I'd revert to normal, but I haven't changed back. Like my cells have been rearranged. I have been enchanted by some sort of fairy tale kiss. Nuts, right?"

"Of course not." Skye wagged her head.

"Crazy? Not at all. But boy am I jealous." Summer sighed.

"For years I've read in romances that time stopped or the earth shook as each author created descriptions of that one special kiss bestowed by a magical soul mate. I enjoy the fantasies, but give me a break. I've done my share of kissing and the floor always stayed still, time never stopped and fireworks only exploded on the 4th of July. Until last night. When Jack took my face in his hands and lowered his lips to mine, well... I can't describe it." Bree's cheeks flamed at the memory. "It just can't be real."

"Of course it's real." Skye knitted her brows. "Look at Mom and Dad. Magical fairy tale kisses all the way."

He's only here a few more days. "All the same… What good is talking about this? Nothing can come of it." Bree rose to her feet and brushed the sand off her seat and the backside and her legs.

She grasped Summer's outstretched hand and towed her upright. "Let's finish our walk and talk about anything else, please."

"How about those Yankees?" Summer cast Bree a deadpan expression.

Bree burst out laughing.

"Really. What are you going to do about Jack?" Skye said.

"What can I do? I can't take this seriously no matter how attracted I am to him. He just lost his wife, his daughter is his main focus and he has an aversion to shrinks. He's made that abundantly clear. And I haven't even flirted with telling him about…the legend and all."

"As Mom has proved—the Legend doesn't get in the way of true love. Jack kisses like Prince Charming and knocked you off your feet." Summer smiled at Bree. "I'll bet Jack feels the same way about you."

"That's right. How do you know that Jack isn't every bit as turned around as you are?" Skye touched Bree's hand. "I have a feeling that he was. Maybe even *more* than you. How could he not be after kissing you?"

Bree said, "You're extremely prejudiced. But thank you."

"I have an idea. Why don't we plan the Inn's

signature dinner for two for you guys?"

"That's a great idea, Skye," Summer chimed in. "I haven't been here during one of those dinners for years. The last one I think was for Ed and Edith Kelly. Do you remember how cute they were? It was their sixtieth wedding anniversary, wasn't it?"

"I remember that," Bree said. "It was the summer before I left for college. Remember how we had to help Mr. Kelly over the dunes? It was so beautiful to witness their love. When Dad played the guitar and they danced together Mom and the three of us burst into tears."

"There you go, Bree. Another example of fairy tale love. Now I *really* hate that I have to go back today. I want to be a part of it. Maybe I'll stay one more day."

The romantic dinner suggestion appealed to Bree. But Summer's career took precedence. "I don't want you to get into trouble with your boss over me."

"Trust me. You're not to blame. I'm all excited about this and my mind is made up. I'm in, Skye. Now let's do what we do best—plan."

Her sisters' enthusiasm was contagious. Bree closed her eyes picturing her great grandmother's lace tablecloth billowing in the evening breeze and candles twinkling in hurricane lamps. She imagined that she smelled the vanilla scented candles her mother preferred.

"Jack seems like a meat guy to me, what do you think?"

Summer's crisp, business-like tone broke Bree's reverie. "Does Mom have any of the frozen pizzas left that I sent her last month? I know Jack would love them. He eats Lou Malnati's pizza often at home."

"That's not romantic!" Skye shook her head

rejecting the suggestion. "The menu has to be special."

"Let's not go crazy, OK?" Bree begged. "I think I'm making way too much of this. What if he thinks I'm pushy? Or clingy?"

Appalled, Bree said, "I don't think this is a good idea after all."

"It's perfect," Skye countered. "Don't worry. Summer, Mom and I will take care of everything. You just show up at six wearing that pretty coral dress hanging in the closet."

I'll die of embarrassment if Jack sees this as some sort of seduction scheme. "But…"

"Trust us, OK?" Summer circled her arm around Bree's shoulder.

Skye gazed seaward shading her eyes with her hand. "Oh look! There are my girls, Molly and Holly." She pointed to two dolphins frolicking in the waves near the shore.

Giving her sisters a sly grin, Skye's gaze roved up and down the desolate beach. "No one is around. What do you say we take a quick swim just like old times?"

"I'm up for it."

"Me, too," Bree added needing the distraction.

Bree and Summer clasped each of Skye's outstretched hands, bolted forward and dived into the surf. Breaching the crest of a wave Bree and her sisters joined the dolphins, which playfully nudged the triplets as they swam and surfed: five dolphins cavorting offshore.

Chapter 12

Jack had a sudden urge to gaze out through the glass sliding door. Diverting his attention from his laptop's screen, he squinted seaward. A pod of five dolphins performed so close to the shallows near the Inn that were he on the beach, he might stretch out his arm and touch one. He bounded off his desk chair and raced into Gabriella's room to wake her.

"Hey, sweetheart," he crooned into her ear. "Want to see the dolphins?"

She blinked open her eyes. "Huh?"

He flipped back an edge of her bed covers exposing one of her slender arms. Clasping hold of her hand he tugged gently. "Come on. They're jumping clear out of the water. It's better than the show at the Shedd Aquarium."

She allowed him to fling off her covers and tow her out of bed. Circling a supportive arm around her shoulders he led her toward the door leading to the balcony off her room. Jack slid open the door and ushered her outside.

He shaded his eyes and stared at the radiant sun glint on the water searching for the school of dolphins. "There!" he exclaimed pointing toward the silvery creature leaping out of the sea. A second dolphin's dorsal fin breached the surface and then disappeared as the "jumper" nose-dived into the ocean.

Female laughter sounded seemingly under his feet. Skye came into view on the beach below, followed by Bree and Summer in tandem.

"Hi guys," Skye called out, waving enthusiastically at him and Gabriella. "You should go for a swim. The water's gorgeous this morning."

Jack couldn't tear his eyes away from Bree's beautiful face. He managed to shift his gaze only long enough to take in her slim sexy figure in the black bathing suit, her wet maroon hair slicked back off her face and cascading down her back. What woman could compare to Bree Layton? Her flawless complexion... Her brilliant smile... Even her sisters, virtually two carbon copies, suffered in comparison.

Bree's gaze spun him into a tizzy of longing. Just kissing the woman had ignited the deepest desire he'd ever experienced as if every molecule in his body were stimulated at once. Jack sensed that making love to Bree would redefine completion. One thing for damn sure, the sight of her made him intend to find out.

"Hi, Jack, hi, Ella!" Bree called. "Coming down for breakfast soon?"

It struck Jack that Bree's voice was his second favorite sound in the world next to Gabriella's last night. *God, I want her.*

Gabriella tugged on his hand as if urging him to respond. He smiled at her. "Ready for breakfast?"

At her nod, Jack was about to give a shout out to Bree when his daughter preempted him. "We'll be right there," her bell-toned voice sang out.

From below his balcony the women cheered. Grinning, Jack ducked back inside with Gabriella in tow. Heading through the connecting door into his room he tossed out, "We have time to grab a bite before we head to Corolla to see the wild horses. Sound good?"

She rounded her eyes. "Really? There are wild horses here?"

"Yep." Jack slipped a brochure advertising Wild Horse Adventure Tours off the bedside table and handed it to Gabriella. "Here you go."

Despite his casual interaction with his child, Jack's heart pumped wildly. Hearing her use her voice again after the long spell of muteness had him simultaneously elated and petrified that he'd do something stupid that would plunge her into a vacuum of silence again.

He powered down his laptop, slipped the bulky room key inside the right, side pocket of his shorts, tucked his cell phone in his other side pocket and took a few steps toward the door. Pulling up short he remembered to detour into the bathroom to find the spray can of 50 SPF sunscreen. "Hey sweetheart! Let me put some of this stuff on you first."

****

Relaxed and happy, Jack shaved for the second time that day. Surveying his face in the mirror, he deemed himself presentable. He shook a couple drops of aftershave into his palm, pressed both palms together and then patted his cheeks dispersing the minty, citrus scent of Armani Sport Code. Sophia had loved the stuff claiming it made her hot. She had kept him amply supplied. He hoped that Bree's taste ran along the same lines.

As promised, when Skye and Summer had corralled him downstairs after returning from the wild horses adventure, Skye had appeared at his door a half hour ago to whisk his daughter away for the evening while Jack and Bree indulged in the Inn's Signature Beach Dinner—whatever that entailed. The two apparently amused Layton sisters had informed him that the price of the dinner for two would be added to his lodging charges since he was the loser in a race with Bree. Small price to pay no matter how high the bill. He had anticipated the evening with relish. Jack had found it impossible to stop thinking about Bree no matter how much vacation fun he had with Gabriella all day.

Dressed in light gray chinos and a powder blue Polo shirt, Jack was ready five minutes before the scheduled dinner bell at eight. He left his room, traversed the hallway and bounded down the back stairs. Through the kitchen windows, he spied glimmering illumination just beyond the dunes.

Curious, he headed outside. The temperature was ideal for outdoor dining and a soft breeze rustled the palm trees surrounding the Inn. Pinpoint stars dotted the royal blue, twilight sky and acoustic guitar music drifted on the light air.

Jack crested the dune, catching sight of Bree standing near the water's edge. His gaze riveted on her back, he slogged in the sand on the downslope. The long skirt of the coral, strapless dress she wore fluttered around her legs. Close to Jack's position on the beach, a snow white lace cloth adorned a round table centered beneath a tented canopy of ivory satin. Fairy lights twined around the canopy's four legs and lined the square edges of the canopy's material. A semi-circle of Tiki torches posted in the sand around the canopy cast flickering light on Bree's hair and bare shoulders.

Enchanted, Jack approached her, laid his hands on

her shoulders and kissed the side of her neck gently. He drank in her garden scent and thrilled at the baby soft skin beneath his lips. She leaned back against his chest with a sigh and he folded his arms around her waist. The guitar instrumental gelled into a melody in Jack's consciousness: *Just the Way You Look Tonight.*

"If I could carry a tune, I'd sing that song to you. You look beautiful tonight, Bree."

She pirouetted within the circle of his arms, stood on tiptoe and pecked a kiss on his lips. Smiling up at him, she said, "You look gorgeous yourself. Hungry?"

"Sure."

Bree took his hand and they strolled toward the table. Ducking under the canopy, Jack pulled out a white, fabric-skirted chair for her and Bree sat down. He tucked her closer to the table and then took a seat in the chair opposite the glowing woman with luminous emerald eyes. The music continued, but for that moment Jack was content not to question its source or say anything at all. A strong conviction took hold that those stars overhead had somehow aligned perfectly four days ago to draw him and his daughter to this place. So Gabriella could find her voice. And Jack could find his...Bree.

Enthralled, he rested his arms on the table, elbows down, the palms of his hands up inviting her touch. She didn't disappoint him. Her tiny hands covered his, an innocent touch that carried a far from innocent jolt to Jack's libido. The music ended and a muffled basso voice called out, "Any requests?"

Jack shot Bree a quizzical gaze.

"My dad," she responded under her breath.

He snorted a laugh. "Where is he?" he whispered.

117

"On the far side of the porch. He rigged up a wireless mic with the speaker over there." She pointed in the direction of the sand dune.

Jack swiveled in his chair and squinted back towards the building. Mike waved at him with one hand, the other resting on the neck of the guitar hanging from a neck strap. Waving back, Jack cupped one hand around his mouth and hollered, "Thanks, Mike. Great playing. We're good for now."

Kay, Skye and Summer emerged through the sliding door out onto the deck, three beauties toting covered, silver serving dishes. Jack repositioned in his chair to face Bree. "What's on the menu?"

"You'll see. We guessed what you might like. Hope we hit the mark."

He eyed the red wine glasses already half full with ruby red liquid at their place settings and picked up the uncorked bottle on the table. "Paso Robles 2010 Cabernet. Beef?"

"Yep."

By then the ladies had reached the table. The sisters placed domed covered plates before Bree and Jack. Kay set the lidded chafing dish that she carried in a holder, lit the Sterno candle beneath it and then ringed the holder with a wind guard. The three women clasped the metal knobs atop the dish covers and removed them simultaneously with a flourish, revealing what looked like sumptuous food. "Enjoy," Kay said herding her daughters back to the Inn.

"The chafing dish held medium rare, slices of Chateaubriand—enough to feed Jack, Bree, Gabriella and *all* the Laytons, probably with leftovers to spare. His and Bree's plates held identical fare: a twice baked potato; a half of a beefsteak tomato, grilled and crusted with parmesan cheese; and asparagus spears laced with a creamy sauce.

Jack dipped a fingertip into the sauce, brought it to his mouth and licked it clean. "Hollandaise. Delicious. This all looks delicious."

He picked up the serving fork in front of the chafing dish and speared a slice of steak. Hovering it over Bree's plate, "May I?"

"Thank you."

Jack served himself two slices and dug in. Two thirds into cleaning his plate he said, "Really great. Can you cook like this?"

Bree chewed and swallowed a bite. "I'm a fair cook. Never really tried to go all out like Mom. I think I'd need a family as inspiration to test my cooking skills. Dinner for one at home is kind of grab and eat."

"Same for me when I was single. Now the cook..." He grimaced.

"What?"

"Did that sound pompous? It wasn't my idea. Actually it was a prerequisite of Sophia's for marriage." He grimaced.

Bree sat back in her seat and regarded him, a serene expression in her exquisite eyes. "Not pompous, especially now with Ella. One less thing to worry about. Hopefully, the cook provides her with nutritious meals?"

"Very skilled at concealing nutrition in her dishes."

"Worth her weight in gold."

A few guitar chords sounded.

"Hmm. I believe there's the possibility of dancing with this dinner extravaganza," she said wryly.

"Interested?"

"Bring it on."

Bree stood and signaled in the direction of the inn with a wave of her arm drawing Jack's gaze to the swell of her breasts in the strapless dress and her enticing cleavage above the elastic holding the garment up. *One tug on the hem? Maybe two?*

Mike bounded off the porch and loped through the sand over to the canopy. As if he were a professional hired for the occasion, he lowered his eyes and began playing a very expert acoustic rendition of *What a Wonderful World.*

Jack offered Bree his hand and when she accepted by gently linking her hand in his, he led her to a spot outside of the torch glare on the damp sand hardened by the tides. With Bree in his arms Jack waltzed to the rhythms of tumbling surf, strumming melody and his pounding heart. Wanting so much more than ending a dance, Jack escorted Bree back to the table.

"Dessert?" Mike said.

"I couldn't," Bree said.

"Me either," Jack echoed.

"OK. Good night kids."

The big man lumbered homeward and Jack turned his attention to Bree. She grinned at him as if she had a secret.

"What?"

"A pretty night."

"Damned near perfect."

"Ever swim in the ocean by moonlight?"

He narrowed his eyes and held her gaze. "Not that I recall."

"Want to now?"

"Aren't you afraid of sharks...or whatever?"

"Off Cape Hatteras maybe. Not so much here."

"And then there's the lack of bathing suits."

"Well *that's* not a problem."

She rose from her seat and in one fluid motion shed the dress. *One tug, not two.*

Bree stood before him in a white strapless bra and white bikini underpants.

Jack whipped his Polo shirt up off his body before he was fully upright on the sand. He unbuttoned his pants, unzipped and slid the chinos into a pool around his ankles. She grabbed his hand and yanked him into a run in a southerly direction along the sand. Outside of the reach of Tiki torches and fairy lights and into the shadows she veered seaward.

Laughing he sloshed into the tide pool at her side, released her hand and dove into the first adequate wave. Submerged, Jack was as turned around underwater as he was in Bree's thrall sitting under a satin canopy. He broke the surface at the same time that she did, rearing his head back and shaking off the cool water. She bobbed in his direction and clung to him, her arms a slippery necklace. He kissed her—the taste of salt, the undulation of the sea and the faint smell of lilacs the most potent aphrodisiac he'd ever known.

Breathless, he held her almost weightless body in his arms as the gentle surf rocked them up, down, side to side.

"I want you so much, Jack."

Absolutely exactly what he wanted to hear. "I want you this minute."

He drew her closer and hopped to keep above the swell of a rolling wave. He wanted nothing more than to take Bree to bed. But here? Her parents and sibs? His little girl? "But your family's home isn't the place."

She blew out a puff of air, maybe as frustrated as he. "You're right. Let's go dry off. And maybe finish that wine."

"Dessert might not be a bad idea," he said towing her closer to shore. "I hope you'll want to see me in Chicago."

Sloshing out of the surf at his side, she grinned up at him. "That's a great idea."

Chapter 13

A mug of tea in hand, Bree leaned against the armrest of the Adirondack chair. In the open air, her hair flew in her face fragmenting her seaward view. Last night was everything she had hoped for and more, she thought. And yet insecurity dogged her. Was Jack as close to surrendering his soul as she? When he contained the nuclear attraction between them and suggested that they see each other in Chicago, her heart had leapt at the prospect of more than a week with Jack.

But alone in her bed sleep evaded her. A cloud of doubt dulled the euphoria. *Was the over the top romantic dinner a turn off? Was she wrong to give Skye free rein? Did every woman in love obsess about every little thing?*

This was no beach vacation crush. Jack had ignited an all-encompassing passion within Bree. Last night was perfect, whether he felt the same way or not.

Kay climbed the wooden deck stairs. "Good morning, sweetheart. You're up early. I hoped you would sleep in today." Leaning against the newel post, she raised each foot in turn and briskly brushed off sand. "Is everything all right?"

"Everything is wonderful. Thank you for last night. You outdid yourself with that dinner."

"I hope you and Jack were OK with Daddy's guitar serenades. He was determined to make the evening special, and I didn't have the heart to discourage him." Kay arched her eyebrows, her eyes dancing.

Bree chuckled. "The music was great, too."

"Skye and Summer really enjoyed planning it all for you. I better get inside and help with breakfast." She headed towards the sliding glass door.

"Mom, can you fall in love in a few days? I mean, true love. Lasting love?"

Kay reversed direction and returned to Bree's side. She wrapped her arm around Bree's shoulders. "Oh, honey. Are you falling in love with Jack?"

"I think so." Her heart swelled just hearing his name. "I know so."

"I'm so happy for you."

"Really? You don't think I'm crazy to feel this way so fast? This has never happened to me before."

"Of course not; you only meet your soul mate once. And when that happens, everything changes." Kay laughed and gave Bree's arm a gentle pat. "That first quick glance at your dad, and I knew in a split-second that my soul had waited just for him." Kay closed her eyes and a soft smile bloomed on her lips. "I'm so lucky that we met. My fondest wish for each of you girls is that you may find your one and only."

Jack is my one and only. "I think I have, Mom." Bree brushed a kiss on Kay's cheek.

She linked arms with her mother and went inside.

"Look at my beautiful girls." Mike cast an admiring smile at Bree and Kay as he stood at the stove wielding a spatula in a sizzling pan. Savory aromas of onions and peppers permeated the air.

Bree sauntered behind him and swept her arms around his waist. "Thank you for the dinner music,

Daddy." She rested her cheek on the solid warmth of his muscular back.

"Anything for you, princess. You know that you're my favorite." He chuckled and tossed the omelet over in the pan like a professional chef.

"Oh yum. Your Southwest omelets are the best. That noise you hear is my stomach growling." Bree wandered behind the counter and perched on a high stool.

Mike folded the omelet into the chafing dish on the counter and then returned the pan to the stove. A timer chimed. Kay donned two lobster shaped pot holders and removed three cast iron pans of corn bread from the oven, setting each in turn atop trivets on the counter.

Summer floated into the room clad in a perfectly cut, slate gray power suit and heels. "I can feel my waistband getting tighter just breathing in here." She filled a large mug at the coffee urn.

"You look spectacular," Bree said inspecting Summer's outfit, lingering longingly on her sister's black designer pumps. "Those shoes are to die for."

"Thanks. I'm going straight into the office from here." She gulped from the mug and then gave a contented sigh. "I wanted to get on the road early, but the minute I smelled Daddy's omelets, I was a goner. As usual, I'll hit the gym hard every day after work for the next week at *least*."

She took another hit of caffeine. Summer riveted her gaze on Bree. Widening her eyes, she grinned. "Everything go well after dinner last night?"

Bree caught the insinuation and bit back a smile. "Yep," she said simply. "Thanks for pitching in with Skye."

"It was fun. We had a great time with Ella. She has a unique relationship with Skye, but who doesn't? Skye is special."

"She is. But don't forget—I think you're pretty special, too."

Skye breezed into the kitchen, her multi-colored maxi skirt swirling around her slim legs with each stride. "What a beautiful morning. Did you see the pink clouds? Just amazing. I had to tear myself away from my easel. Daddy that smells good."

"Sit down and help yourselves. I hear our guests coming down the stairs." Mike flipped two more omelets into the chafing dish. Kay expertly cut the cornbread into pie shaped slices and served her daughters.

Ella ran into the dining area. Bree's heartbeat skittered as Jack emerged through the archway trailing his little girl at a brisk pace. His soulful eyes scanned the room's occupants and honed in on Bree. A broad smile creased laugh lines on his handsome face. She beamed at him, happier than she thought possible.

"Morning, everyone. I'm becoming repetitive, but something smells amazing in here." Jack lifted the lid off a chafing dish.

"Help yourself." Kay bustled over to the service counter, sliced more cornbread and placed a huge wedge on his plate.

Mike smiled at Ella. "Princess, would you like a cheese omelet or pancakes?"

Ella glanced furtively at Skye's plate before replying, "An omelet, please." Mike provided Ella with her meal, topped off the coffee mugs, and then took his place at the head of the table.

"You play a mean guitar, Mike and you have a great voice. I enjoyed your music a lot. And the food was amazing. It was a perfect night." Jack's eyes were riveted on Bree. "A night I won't ..."

****

"Anybody home?" A deep voice boomed cutting Jack off midsentence.

An imposing figure seemingly filled the archway between the kitchen and front parlor. "Where's my girl?"

"Vinnie!" Bree jettisoned off her seat toward the man. "What are you doing here?"

"I had to check on you, hon."

Hon? Jack tightened the grip on his fork.

"I haven't heard from you in a week. Don't you return calls?" He brought a hand from behind his back revealing a bouquet of at least three dozen yellow roses. He presented the flowers to Bree.

"Oh my. These are gorgeous." She buried her nose in the blossoms and sighed. "They smell good, too."

"Not as good as you." The guy towered over Bree and had to bend at the waist to bus her cheek with a kiss.

Jack's blood pressure soared at her casual receipt of another man's affection. She carried the flowers towards the sink and the interloper waltzed into the room seemingly very comfortable approaching Bree's family.

"Kay, Mike so good to see you again."

Mike rose from his seat to shake Vinnie's hand. "Join us." He pulled out the chair opposite Jack for the stranger. *Well, obviously not to the Laytons...just one of the family.*

"Have a seat. I'll get you a plate," Mike said.

Vinnie shrugged out of his jacket and folded it over the back of the chair. His skin tight gray t-shirt, and leg sculpting jeans displayed a gym rat physique. A shoulder holster completed the macho look.

****

Bree filled a vase at the sink and smiled as Summer's eyes roved over every delicious inch of the man. She would have to warn Summer. Vinnie had the body of an athlete, the face of a choir boy and charm aplenty. Problem was, he was acutely aware of his effect on women and used it to his advantage; she wouldn't let her sister become just another Carlucci conquest.

"I see you're packing, Vin," Summer quipped.

"I am. And I have my gun strapped on, too." He gifted her with a wicked smile, and Summer's bawdy laughter sounded.

"Where are my manners?" Bree sat back down at the table. "Vinnie, this is Jack Tremonti and his beautiful daughter, Gabriella. Jack and Ella, this is my friend Vincente Carlucci."

"Hello, little lady. I'm pleased to meet you." Vinnie reached his right arm across the table, clasped Ella's tiny hand and kissed it dramatically.

She giggled. "You're just like prince charming."

Stone-faced, Jack accepted the proffered handshake.

Bree wondered what was wrong with Jack as she unsuccessfully tried to catch his eye.

Vinnie sat at the table and dug into the food that Mike had provided. Demolishing the omelet in seconds he proclaimed, "Man, that was good. Honey, you told me about the breakfasts here at the Inn, but you didn't do them justice.

"What do you do, Jack?" Vinnie leaned back in his chair, his coffee mug in hand.

"Computers," Jack barked.

"Oh you're a tech geek."

Bree winced. But Jack didn't give Vinnie a reaction to his dig other than a tightening of his jaw and a frosty glare. Training his eyes on the gun, Jack said, "I take it you're a cop."

"FBI."

"Vinnie is responsible for Bree's bullet wound," Skye chimed in, her voice strident, accusatory.

Bree's stomach fell. She hated how much her family had hurt when her involvement with Vinnie's case hadn't gone well.

"Yeah, I heard about how you got her hurt," Jack spat out.

Vinnie frowned. "God, no. I could never hurt my girl."

"You might as well have pulled the trigger. You put her in harm's way," Skye persisted.

"How many times do I have to apologize, Skye? You know I would do anything to change what happened."

Bree had absolved Vinnie from blame from the outset of her involvement with his case. The profiling had fascinated her and it was her idea to accompany him to the interview where she had been hurt. He had tried to make amends for not protecting her enough by sending a private plane for her family so they could be at the hospital by the time she got out of surgery and had paid all their expenses while they stayed in

Chicago... But Skye felt things more deeply than anyone. The pain of the gunshot wound hurt Skye as much as Bree, maybe more.

"I have to head out. I have a long drive ahead of me." Summer pushed her chair back and rose from the table. "As much as I would like to stay and listen to Vin grovel."

Summer put her plate in the sink and then returned to the table. She kissed their parents and then doled out kisses to Bree and Skye. "Call me tonight, Bree. Great seeing you, Vin. Oh, and don't put my sister in jeopardy again or you'll have to deal with me."

"Promise."

"Drive safe. Call us when you get home, please."

"Will do, Mom. Love you guys."

"Are you here for a vacation, Vinnie?" Mike asked filling the vacuum of Summer's abrupt departure.

"Sort of. Had to see my girl and finally try this wonderful food." He grinned at Bree.

Jack's eyes darkened.

"Cut the sh...uh, sausage." Bree curbed her tongue. Ella hung on every word at the table. "You didn't come all this way for an omelet. What's going on? Another case?"

Skye practically bolted out of her chair. "Let's go see if the shell ornaments we've made have dried, Ella. I have them on the deck off my room."

Ella popped up from her seat to join Skye, apparently eager to follow her idol anywhere.

Skye doesn't want Ella to hear what Vinnie might say. Soft soul that she is, she probably doesn't want to hear it, either.

"I can't get into it with you. But I really did want to

see you." Vinnie put his napkin on the table and drained his coffee mug.

"Does it have anything to do with the van abandoned on the bridge with the seven million dollars' worth of drugs?" Mike said. "I heard the driver didn't survive. Did you find out his identity?"

"Sorry, Mike, but I can't answer that. I wish I could. I've put one member of your family in danger. Lesson learned. It won't happen again."

"That's good to know," Jack growled as he shoved away from the table. "Try not to get your girl shot again." He stormed out of the room.

"How long will you be in town?" Kay asked. "Would you like a room here?"

"I'm not sure how long I'll be here and I already have a room booked at Whale House Motel. I don't want to impose."

"Nonsense. Of course you'll stay with us. Mike could you please check Vinnie in and show him to his room?" Kay said.

Mike's brow knit, but he didn't question his wife. He led Vinnie out of the room, leaving Kay and Bree alone at the table.

"That went well." Kay burst out laughing,

"How can you laugh, Mom? What just happened? Skye's upset and Jack just stormed off, and you just let Vinnie stay here. What were you thinking?"

"I was thinking a jealous man does not like his soul mate being called someone else's girl."

Chapter 14

Bree cleared the dishes from the table, working in tandem with her mother at the kitchen sink when Vinnie's voice boomed from behind her. "Am I too late to ask for another mug of coffee?"

"Of course not." Kay shooed Bree away releasing her from KP.

Bree snagged a clean mug from the cabinet and filled it for her friend; black and piping hot, the way he liked it.

"Here you go." She handed him the mug as he tilted his head in the direction of the deck.

Interpreting the cue, she stepped towards the sliding door, unlatched the lock and swept the door open. Vinnie ambled through the doorway and Bree followed him, shoving the slider closed behind her. Outdoors, the constant breeze and ever-moving ocean sounded a muted roar in her ears.

She swept a tendril of hair away from her mouth and tucked it behind her ear. "So you're investigating the drug trafficking, right? Are you here alone? Or is your partner in town, too? Any way I can help?"

Squinting against sun glare, Bree peered up at Vinnie's profile. He gazed seaward, his buzz cut, sable hair unmoving in the wind. "You really want to hear about the case I'm building? And God forbid, help?"

He faced her frowning. "At least one of your sisters

will try to kill me." He gave her a crooked grin. "Maybe both."

Bree dismissed his concern with a wag of her head. "I know that they have long since exonerated you from blame no matter how protective my sisters act. I also know that you won't expose me to danger again. But..."

Bree leveled her gaze directly into his robin egg blue eyes. "You didn't just happen to our Inn this morning. First of all, you know I help my family open for the season the week before Memorial Day *every* year. Second—I'm certain you think I can help you or you wouldn't be staying here. So spill..."

Vinnie narrowed his eyes, apparently mulling over Bree's assessment. "All... right," he conceded as if she had left him no choice. Bree was positive that no arm-twisting on her part was ever necessary and that he had premeditated her response to his unexpected appearance from the minute he left the Field Office in New York.

"I'm working advance surveillance of a couple suspects—yes, involving the confiscated drugs from the van on the bridge that your dad brought up at breakfast. Depending on the connections I establish, we'll bring in a tactical unit, including my partner."

"OK. How do I fit in?"

"You might have knowledge of the suspects."

"Really? I don't see how. I haven't lived here since I was a teenager and my socializing on OBX when I visit is confined to my family. I'm positive we haven't crossed paths with any drug runners."

"This may go back way back." He took a sip of coffee. "Do you know anything about Wyatt & Sons Marine? Or Windward Deep Sea Fishing Charters?"

"Sure. We have brochures in the parlor for both companies. They have the largest fleets on the island. Wyatt has both a commercial fishing and charter operations. Windward has operated strictly charter boats since I was a kid. Wyatt expanded into charter boat operations sometime in the last ten years. I can check with my parents if you need exact information. I actually was in the same class in high school as one of the Wyatt boys, Randy. I saw him recently at the store. He's even creepier than when he was in high school. I take it they're suspects."

"Uh huh." Vinnie drained his mug. "The van was headed *off* the Banks. Supply logistics has to involve water vessels; delivery by ship to smaller craft is the most logical. Possibly sea planes, although that's not my first line of investigation."

"Dare County Regional Airport is in Manteo. It can accommodate small jets."

"I'll check it out, but I want to start with the two fishing boat companies."

"I can introduce you to Mr. Wyatt if you want. My dad might know the owners at Windward."

"Thanks." He stooped to set his empty mug down on the deck and then he stood leaning his forearms on the railing. "Any sense of which operation might conceal criminal activities? I have limited coverage from the Coast Guard at this point. As I build the case we'll have leverage to increase their involvement."

"I don't know very much about either operation. If you're asking me if any of the parties might fit a deviant criminal profile, yep. Randy Wyatt fits perfectly. And he takes after his father."

"All right. Let me think about the setup for initial

contact."

"How about I make a reservation for you to charter one of the Wyatt boats? And then drive you over there and introduce you as a VIP guest at the Inn?"

"That wouldn't work. I'd have to follow through and disappear on a boat for the day. There might be some value to that, but I don't want to lose the time."

"Hmmm..." Bree twisted her lips and gazed out to sea considering alternatives.

"What if you make the reservation instead for you and lover boy to go fishing? I'll drive you over there and you can introduce me as a seasonal Inn employee or something?"

The only phrase that Bree heard during Vinnie's half of that exchange was "lover boy". "What the *hell*, Vin? Are you referring to Jackson Tremonti?"

"Yeah...wait. That name rings a bell. Is he with JET?"

"He *is* JET. By the way, I don't think he liked your referring to him as a tech geek."

Vinnie guffawed. "Trust me, hon. He didn't like me at all. What do you think about the fishing charter ploy with him?"

"Well..." Jack and Ella might enjoy the outing. She could make it an adventure for the little girl; teach her how to reel in a fish. I'll check with Jack and let you know later."

"Cool." Vinnie shoved away from the deck railing. "I'm going to drive the area for a few hours. I rented a garish Kelly green car. The last thing it says is, G-man."

Bree snorted a laugh as she turned towards the house. "I'll see you later."

****

Jack pounded furiously on his computer keyboard, more for the release than to finish his work faster. Why had he allowed a woman that he hardly knew take possession of his thoughts? That guy, *that guy*, acted like he owned her. Maybe he did.

But could she behave as passionately with him if this other guy were still in the picture with her? Was he ever in the picture with her? All those yellow roses. Were they her favorite flower? Favorite color? Referring to Bree as "hon" and "my girl". What bullshit.

And the guy had called him a geek? Big deal FBI agent. Wearing a gun to breakfast at The Inn of The Butterflies for God sake. What kind of an asshole does that? And to top it all off, the guy got her shot. Why the hell is she even talking to this jerk?

Frustrated, Jack forced his attention back to the laptop's screen. No use. His attraction to Bree was too complicated, all-consuming. His opinion of her qualities these past five days: genuine sweetness, kindness, honesty, intelligence—snagged on honesty. Was she involved with "Vin"? Or who knows, other men besides him? Had she duped him into believing that what they had together was exclusive, special?

What *did* they have together, anyway? A few explosive kisses and a blood boiling swim in their underwear? Why did that have him spinning fantasies about what they'd do alone in Chicago?

Jack should give up on continuing the relationship with Bree beyond the duration of this trip. Three days were left of his vacation. Surely, he could enjoy time with Gabriella and remain cordial with the Inn keepers' daughter.

Who am I trying to kid? To keep his head straight, he'd have to avoid Bree altogether.

Raising his eyes from the screen, Jack checked on Gabriella in her room. She reclined on the bed, her head propped up on pillows, absorbed in playing a game on her tablet. Despite his inner turmoil, Jack grinned at the sight.

He powered down his laptop and called out to his daughter, "Ready, sweetheart?"

Gabriella tore her eyes away from the screen and glanced at him, jade eyes sparkling. "To climb the dunes?"

"Yep."

She jumped off the bed and raced toward him. Her soft, small hand clasped his and Jack's heart leaped at the connection. "Let's go," she said sweetly.

Regardless of future prospects with Bree, he'd always be grateful that he happened upon the Inn for Gabriella's sake. Jack scooped his keys off the dresser, donned sunglasses and led his little girl out of the room.

Downstairs Jack encountered Kay vigorously wiping off the countertops, and Bree heading inside through the sliding glass door. Vin hulked near the deck railing, his back presented to Jack.

His insecurities fired up again until pleasure at the sheer sight of Bree diverted his train of thought.

Just look at her. Not a trace of makeup. She didn't need it. That beautiful face, her shining eyes...that smile. Everything about her was magic.

"Hey," she said approaching him. "What are you two up to?"

Delight danced in Gabriella's eyes. "Daddy is

taking me to see the biggest sand dunes in the whole United States."

"Oh, you're gonna *love* that," Kay exclaimed. "Take a lot of photos, Jack. The views are stupendous from the top of Jockey Ridge."

"Be sure to look for pieces of fulgurite while you climb," Bree said. "Do you know what that is, Ella?"

At the shake of Gabriella's head, Bree continued, "When lightning hits sand and the conditions are right, glass is created. We've found some amazing formations over the years. Skye even painted an abstract with fulgurite as the subject."

Bree sauntered near Jack, close enough to breathe in her sweet scent and imagine the warmth of her slim arms necklaced around him. "Do you need directions?"

"Nah." He grinned. "I'm pretty set with technology."

Bree beamed at him. "Well, duh."

Her eyes danced as she riveted her gaze on Jack. In the background, Jack spied Vinnie's movement. The guy clomped heavy footfalls along the deck and then disappeared from view. Ever the competitor, Jack's insecurities dissolved. Even if there was something between Vinnie and Bree, what difference did it make? The powerful magnetism he experienced when she was near had to be mutual. He hadn't detected that sexy vibe directed at *Vin*. Whether Bree viewed the other guy as his competition or not, Jack intended to prevail.

"Would you like to come with us?"

A pretty blush bloomed on her milk-white cheeks. "Oh... I don't want to interfere with your time with Ella."

Gabriella, bless her heart, read her father's mind.

"Please come, Bree? We'll have so much fun."

****

Gleeful at the prospect of spending the day with him and his child, whom she truly loved, Bree accepted. "I'd love to come. Let me pack a tote bag first?"

Jack nodded. "We'll wait for you in the car. Take your time."

Bree took a moment to appreciate the rear view of Jack's motion out of the room.

"He's an eyeful, huh?" Kay smiled at Bree, obviously entertained.

"Oh yeah." Bree zipped out to the screen porch, snagged a canvas tote bag off the wall hook and returned to the kitchen. "OK if I pack some sandwiches and fruit?"

"Of course. I'll help."

Hefting the straps of the bulging bag over her shoulder, Bree kissed Kay's cheek and exited the kitchen into the parlor. She chose a pair of sunglasses, oversized white frames with black polka dots, out of a large bowl set on a table near the front entry, flung open the screen door, clattered down the wooden steps, and then strode to the back of Jack's car. The trunk opened with a resounding pop. Bree stowed the picnic lunch and then flattened her palm down on top of the trunk's lid to push it closed.

Rounding the bumper, Bree peered inside the car. Gabriella was seated in the backseat. Her heart leapt in anticipation as she flung open the passenger door and slipped inside the car.

Chapter 15

From her place at the kitchen table, Bree had a panoramic view through the salt streaked windows of the back deck and seascape beyond. She observed the solitary figure huddled on the top step of the wooden staircase. The tiny girl stared straight ahead, her thin arms wrapped around boney legs.

"Look outside, Skye," Bree directed. "Ella's out there alone."

"I didn't get to say goodnight to her last evening." Skye frowned as she drifted towards the window, kneading her lower back with her fingers. "The drive back from Newport News took forever after the exhibition. An accident blocked Route 64 for hours and finally I used back roads to get through. Dad waited up for me as usual, even though he looked so tired, and I begged him not to worry so much. He said there was a chain reaction but no one was hurt."

"Yes, we were there. It was terrible." Bree rubbed her eyes trying to soothe the sting from lack of sleep. The scene had replayed in her mind all night.

Skye whipped around and regarded Bree, wide-eyed. "Who's 'we'? Was anyone hurt?"

"We're all fine. Jack invited me to come with him and Ella on a Jockey Ridge hike yesterday afternoon. But we never made it there. I sat upfront with Jack. Ella sang along with me to a Taylor Swift song on the radio.

She was probably giggling more than singing. It was so awesome to see the change in her. Jack steered into the left turn lane across from the Jockey Ridge entrance and stopped behind a rusty pickup truck. The driver of this clunker ahead of us didn't even slow down. He hit the gas and jerked left trying to beat oncoming traffic.

"It was awful watching his misjudgment. There was nothing we could do to stop it. The cars crashed one after the other as if in slow motion. The sound of screeching tires, glass breaking and metal crunching was just horrible."

Bree gave her head a shake to dispel the mental images and echoes of the crash.

Knitting her brow, Skye trained glistening eyes on her sister. "I can't stand that you were almost involved."

"I know. It gives me chills to think about it. I grabbed my cell phone and called the police while Jack jumped out of the car to see if he could help."

"Thank God you were all unhurt."

"Well, that's the thing. Ella wasn't hurt physically, but she was in a terrible state. I climbed into the back seat to hold her. She dissolved in tears and repeatedly called for her mom. Skye, it broke my heart that she undoubtedly relived the accident that took her mom's life.

"Luckily, old Mr. Jenkins charged out of the truck, not a scratch on him and bellowed at the guy who hit him. Then that driver bolted out of his car and yelled back at Jenkins practically nose to nose.

"Ella couldn't help but notice since they were making so much noise and she was totally distracted. I thought the scene was pretty comical and I laughed out loud. I hoped Ella might join in. She didn't, but at least she stopped crying."

"Mr. Jenkins is like a hundred years old," Skye said. "He shouldn't be driving."

"Tell me about it. Anyway, Jack gave up refereeing the two idiots yelling in the middle of the road and came back to the car. The cops showed up at the same time. Good thing. Because Jack only had to glance at Ella to imagine what was going on in her head."

Bree and Skye turned their attention back to Ella, still unmoved from her perch on the step. "I co-piloted with directions to the beach road from the backseat. When we returned here, Ella launched out of the car and raced upstairs. Jack followed her. He came down for a dinner tray and they ate in their rooms last night."

"Did he say anything about her condition?"

"Yes. I wasn't there, but he spoke with Mom. He described Ella as calm and subdued. He said that she didn't want to talk about the accident, but she spoke freely about other subjects. So she hasn't regressed."

"Thank God for that. Where's Jack now?"

Bree pointed upwards as she rose from her seat. "He was out there with Ella up until a few minutes ago. He burst in here on a mission for sunscreen. I've kept an eye on her while he went upstairs."

She strolled over to the counter and fixed a mug of tea. "Want some?"

Skye nodded and Bree repeated the task. She toted a steaming mug in each hand and then set them on the table. Seated next to her sister, she sipped tea and let her thoughts drift to the beginning of yesterday: Jack's thrilling body language sparking Bree's elation in his nearness.

Gazing at Ella possessively, Bree marveled that in a matter of days she had come to view her as her own. Just like she viewed Ella's father. *My Jack.*

What would loving him in every way be like? Could he share his daughter with her? Could she share her secrets with him?

Skye touched Bree's arm softly. "I think we need to do something today to take her mind off the accident."

"I agree. Any suggestions?"

Skye pursed her lips and narrowed her eyes. "I have an idea. Let me check with Bic to see if she has an opening for us." Skye tapped numbers on her phone.

Jack strode into the kitchen holding a spray can of sunscreen.

"What's up?" He asked as he grabbed a mug off the counter and filled it with coffee.

"I think Skye is making an appointment for Ella to have a little pampering."

Skye gave Bree a thumbs up. "Bic has time for us. Is it okay if we steal Ella for a couple hours this morning, Jack?"

"I think pampering Ella is a great idea. I'll go, too."

His gaze lit on Bree and he cast her a wry smile.

Bree did a double-take. "Really? You realize that we're talking about a nail salon, right?"

"What? Don't I look like a man who appreciates a mani-pedi?" He smirked.

Bree snorted. "Actually, you look like a man who would run in the opposite direction at the mere mention."

His eyes danced. "Why do you think they call it MAN-icure?"

She snorted, amused. "I'm surprised you even know the phrase mani-pedi."

"Honestly, I've never been to a nail salon in my life." Jack grinned looking boyish, playful, sexy as hell. "But I'm the father of a young lady. I should do this for her."

Bree smiled. "You're a good guy, Mr. Tremonti."

"Thank you, Miss Layton." In two strides, he reached Bree's place at the table. Tipping a finger under her chin, he lowered his head and tilted her head upward to meet his lips. His kiss seared, branded her while her limbs seemingly liquefied. As Skye hooted, he softly withdrew leaving Bree shaky and yearning.

His grin dripped with male confidence. "I'll go collect Gabriella," he tossed out nonchalantly in motion towards the door.

****

Settled in the back seat of Skye's Jeep, Jack teased Ella.

"I think I want purple nail polish," he said without the slightest hint of sarcasm, prompting bursts of laughter from Bree and Skye.

"Daddy, you can't get purple nail polish."

"Why not?"

"Because only girls get purple nail polish."

"Well, I have my heart set on Polly Want a Cracker Purple. All the guys at work will be jealous."

Bree turned to face Jack in the back seat and met with his mischievous grin. He wagged his eyebrows at her.

Parked in a spot outside Bic's Nail Spa, four doors swung open and then slammed shut as the passengers left the car. Entering the salon, the group was surrounded by the proprietor, Bic and her three daughters. Skye and Bree hugged and kissed the women in greeting and then introduced Jack and Ella to their longtime friends.

Bic directed Jack and Ella to side by side pedicure thrones toward the back of the spa.

Bree and Skye remained upfront by the manicure stations chatting with the three women to afford father and daughter alone time.

Only partially immersed in her friends' conversations, Bree kept an eye on Jack and Ella. The girl's bubbly laughter as Bic painted Jack's toenails would resound in Bree's mind long after she returned home. Jack's departure loomed. The realization brought a sharp pang of dread. The prospect of daily life without Jack and Ella loomed empty...lonely.

Skye's cell phone trilled.

"It's Mom," she concluded glancing at the screen. "I better take this call. Excuse me."

She left the salon and paced the sidewalk in front of the shop, phone to her ear. Skye appeared animated throughout the conversation, and then she smiled broadly turning back towards the spa.

"What's up?" Bree asked as Skye came back into the salon.

"Kirsten called the Inn and Mom took the call. Some of her people backed out on her this morning for an engagement and she asked for help. What do you think? We could ask Jack to come, too, or bring him home on our way. We have to be at Jeannette's Pier in a half hour if we're going to do this."

"I'm in. It looks like Bic is done with them. Perfect timing."

****

Skye explained Kirsten's job as they drove out of the parking lot. "We have time to drop you off at the Inn if you don't want to be a part of this."

"What do you think, sweetheart?" Jack posed to Ella.

"I want to go, too, Daddy."

"Yes!" Skye exclaimed. "It's going to be a lot of fun."

Bree shifted around and draped an arm over the passenger seat's headrest regarding Jack and Ella. "Have you ever been part of a flash mob?"

Both wagged their head, no, but Ella chimed in, "I saw one on TV once."

"Good. Then you have a general idea about this. We're going to meet Kirsten in the lot across from the Pier and she'll explain exactly what she wants us to do. I've taken part before when Kirsten was in town directing, and I loved it. I think you will, too."

"I'm glad I got my toe nails painted for the occasion." Jack jutted his foot through the two front seats, his flip-flop dangling over the console. He wiggled his toes showcasing his purple-tipped nails.

Bree hooted a laugh and slapped a love tap on his ankle.

When they arrived at Jeanette's Pier, Bree noted the cluster of people gathered in the park across the street. Skye parked near the group and then led Bree, Jack and Ella over to Kirsten who doled out hugs and asserted, "I can't thank you enough."

"No problem. We're glad to be a part of something so romantic," Bree said.

Kirsten checked her watch and called everyone

together. "Listen up, people. We don't have much time.

"Skye, you've helped me before, so I want you to start. Wait for my signal. I'll stand at the end of the pier. When I raise a yellow card over my head, you start the music. Ted, you and your group should join in when I hold up an orange card."

She continued giving instructions to subsequent groups and then asked Skye to follow her to the trunk of her car.

Equipped with a large Bluetooth speaker, Kirsten's iPod, sunglasses and a huge towel, Skye proceeded to the beach to set up. Jack reached into the trunk and loaded his arms with chairs, a blanket and some beach toys. Shepherding Ella, Bree accompanied Jack across the street, through the parking lot and onto the beach. Ella skipped between them, her black locks blowing behind her in the wind, practically vibrating with excitement.

A group of adults and children positioned on blankets under beach umbrellas near the pier. Kids on the beach dug in the sand with gaily-colored plastic shovels. Skye had set up close to the water's edge—the perfect vantage point to observe Kirsten and wait for her signal.

Jack stripped off his shirt. He lay down on a striped beach towel, sunglasses concealing his eyes, ankles crossed as if snoozing. Bree drank in the delicious sight tempted to glide her hand over the muscled contours of his body. She savored the sensual fantasy inwardly as she sat on a towel next to Ella and joined her digging holes in the sand.

Bree caught movement in the corner of her eye and shifted her gaze with minimal head movement to check it out.

"Here they come," she whispered. "Don't turn your head yet, Ella. The girl has long blonde hair and the boy is in blue bathing trunks." Bree circled a hand in the sand. "Pretend you're looking here in the sand and then glance in the direction of the parking lot."

Ella followed Bree's directions. "I see them. They're putting a blanket down."

Jack rolled over, propped up on his elbows and snuck a peek.

"He looks nervous." Bree's breath caught in her throat as Jack's warm hand covered her kneecap.

"Nervous? He looks scared to death." He chuckled and trailed his fingers over her knee, caressed her lower thigh.

He flashed a wicked grin at Bree's sharp intake of breath.

The next instant Kirsten hoisted a yellow card over her head and the flash was on.

Skye stooped down and hit play on the iPod. Bruno Mars's song *Marry You* blared out of the speakers. Skye danced gracefully. Uninvolved beachgoers stared at her opened mouthed. Proud of her lovely, uninhibited sister, Bree beamed.

Skye was a solo performer a few minutes more and then Kirsten kicked things into gear lifting various colored cards over her head, one after the other. When the blue card went up, Ella popped up before Bree or Jack and perfectly mimicked Skye's movements. Jack wrapped his arms around Bree and swayed with the music. Elation and deep gratitude blossomed inside Bree as she immersed in the special moment—this place, this happy event, this amazing man holding her tightly.

The young couple "of honor" sat on their blanket and surveyed the scene, wide-eyed. The girl's tinkling laughter rode the sea breeze. She hopped up, reached out her hand to her boyfriend and tugged him to his feet. The pair joined in the dance.

Skye led the next phase of the flash. She stopped dead in her tracks, switched off the music and pointed toward the pier.

"Jack, let go," Bree said. "We have to point in a second."

He spun her in a semi-circle and drew her to his side with one arm. "I can point with one hand," he joked.

Bree leaned toward him, sheltered and happy. Bree, Jack and Ella raised their arms and pointed to Jeanette's Pier. In sequence, the other dancers followed suit. All eyes trained on a row of people lining the pier who with dramatic slow motion, hoisted cards overhead spelling, WILL YOU MARRY ME, NATALIE?

The young girl gasped and clamped one hand over her mouth as her boyfriend lowered to one knee before her, a ring box in his upturned palm. "I love you, Natalie. Will you marry me?" he boomed.

Tears streaming, she nodded, spurring her brand new fiancé to stand erect and place a sun sparkling ring on her finger.

"Will you have dinner with me tonight?" Jack said softly, his warm breath tingling against Bree's ear.

The lady of the moment regarded her be-ringed left hand as if wonderstruck and then she threw her arms around the proposer's neck voicing a resounding, "Yes," as Bree echoed the same response to Jack's invitation.

****

The crowd erupted into applause and cheers. Bree swiped tears from under her eyes, noticing the majority of women behaving the same way. A family entourage, toting coolers, streamed onto the beach having hidden up on the pier until the proposal finished. Kirsten and her team handed out plastic champagne glasses, filled from the contents of the coolers. The children were supplied with cans of soda.

Natalie's father, evidenced by a baseball cap lettered DAD, raised his class, "Welcome to our family, Chris," he shouted.

The communal celebration wound down, and the flash mob players strolled off the beach leaving the engaged couple and their family to a private party.

Bree's group grabbed their gear and returned the props to Kirsten's trunk.

"What did you think of that?" Skye asked Ella as she held her hand traversing the parking lot.

"When I get married I want it to be just like that. I want dancing and champagne."

"Uh oh." Jack joked. "Looks like we created a problem for my future son-in-law. How will he ever top that?"

Chapter 16

Jack's reverie on the car ride back to the Inn recast the roles in the elaborate beach proposal. In his mind, *he* lowered to one knee gazing up at Bree's glistening eyes and dazzling smile. Crazy that he would give a moment's thought to the proposition of marriage after knowing a woman for five days, especially after suffering through the dark days of his marriage with Sophia. But Breeze Layton captivated him in a way Sophia never had. He trusted her sweetness and honesty. His potent attraction to her couldn't be denied, or resisted. Without seemingly trying, she had cast a spell over him that he had no intention of resisting.

Skye, Bree and Gabriella chattered and sang songs playing on the radio. Two generations of lovely females whose gentle company Jack felt lucky to share. He had a lot to be grateful for: the happy destiny that brought them to the Inn of the Three Butterflies when Gabriella noticed the sign, and much more. Because of Bree, he had his daughter back, something he had believed impossible. Equally impossible, Bree had restored his faith in love.

When Jack gave his heart, his loyalty was absolute: "I love you," equaled a cast in granite pledge. Sophia... Why dwell on the past on a sunny, carefree day? Especially since his delight in discovering everything about Bree coalesced into certainty. Jack was in no-turning-back love with Breeze Layton.

Stunned that the realization didn't terrify him, Jack grinned as his gaze lingered on the back of Bree's head. Some happy telepathy had her turning around and meeting his eyes. She gifted him with a smile, her jade eyes soft.

Lighthearted, Jack bounded out of the car when they reached the Inn. "Sweetheart, are you up for some beach time?" he tossed out to Gabriella.

"Yes!"

"Let's go change." He sauntered over to Bree standing at the foot of the stairs. "Dinner at seven? Maybe at that seafood place on the Sound?"

She gave him a head nod and a brilliant smile.

Invigorated he bounded up the steps trailing his little girl, almost colliding with the G-man, Vinnie as he entered the parlor. Even that encounter couldn't dampen his high spirits.

Jack hadn't premeditated seducing Bree that evening. The last couple to leave the restaurant after an excellent meal of the day's catch and hours of scintillating conversation, what he had first intended as an appreciative kiss to seal the date's enjoyment before he started up the car, rapidly escalated into a quick fire, sizzling lip lock.

Pretzel twisted over the gearshift console she clung to him, her soft lips fused to his with equal pressure, tongues tangling.

"Jack..." she sighed coming up for air, her lips an inch away from his.

Rational thoughts suspended at her breathless pronouncement of his name. Jack laced his fingers in her hair gently cupping the back of her head and dove in for more, hungry for her and never sated. His hands sought the silken softness of her skin, stroking her bare arms, sliding beneath a bra strap and the material of her filmy summer tank top. Impulse tempted him to caress her breasts or to explore under the gauzy long skirt she wore.

The parking lot was deserted and surely they would appear as nothing more than indistinct shadows should a car pass by on the street. This played through his increasingly aroused senses while Bree's hands stroked the back of his neck, over his shoulders and down his arms, the feather-light trail leaving a flood of white hot sensation in its wake.

The next step would lead to risking indecent exposure charges. Jack reined in desire mustering steely willpower. Forehead to forehead, he caught his breath while clasping both of her slender hands in his.

"I want you so much," he managed.

"Yes," came her soft reply. "Jack, I..."

He had to kiss her again. Just one more time before they returned to their separate rooms at the Inn. A simple goodnight kiss to satisfy him until they could find private time at home in Chicago.

In seconds, he was back at the threshold of zero control. This time Bree possessed the presence of mind to gently pull away. "Jack, I love you," she whispered.

Elation flowered inside him. His heart in his mouth, he said, "I love you, too, Bree."

This brilliant, genuine, stunning woman loved him. His thoughts spun a future with Bree by his side: anniversaries, maybe siblings for Gabriella. Jack smiled at the unspoken, tender fantasy as he fired the car's engine.

****

Jack loved her. Bree could barely control her glee. She had always enjoyed her homecomings. But *this* time? She sang prayers of gratitude in her heart to the Sacred Source for leading her home to find her destined forever with this man—who happened to live in the same city as Bree, even more evidence of predestination.

How she wished that the car headed toward her condo or his penthouse on Lake Shore Drive instead of the Inn teeming with her family. She couldn't wait to get back to Chicago—a desire becoming even more pronounced as Jack pulled up in front of the Inn and Bree spied a tiny flare of light from a seating area on the veranda. Since Vinnie was the only smoker in the house, the deduction that he lay in wait for Bree wasn't much of a stretch.

She could almost feel Jack bristle as they left the car, locked hands and mounted the porch steps. Tempted to completely ignore his presence on the porch and slip past, her perfect evening still intact, Bree opted for a cheery aside instead. "Night, Vin."

Jack grasped the handle and swung open the front door. A step away from eluding possible confrontation between the two men, Vinnie's voice boomed, "Hold up, Breeze. I need to talk with you."

"I'm really tired, Vinnie," she deflected. "Can it wait until morning?"

A waft of cigarette smoke pinched her nostrils as Vinnie neared her. "Just a few minutes, okay?" he persuaded. "It's important."

Jack forged forward evidently turning a deaf ear to

what Vinnie deemed important.

Bree halted in her tracks, a gentle tug back against their interlaced hands. Jack faced her, his face in shadows. "I'll catch up with you upstairs?" she said.

"Sure." He let loose her hand and strode away from her.

Suddenly chilled standing in the doorway, she bit back impatience. "What's up?"

Vinnie took a final drag on his cigarette and then dropped the butt into a soda can, extinguished with a soft hiss. "I want a closer look at your friend's boatyard. Wyatt Marine."

"Whoa. Randy Wyatt is *far* from my friend. Have you checked out both Wyatt and Windward? How about the airport at Manteo?"

"Yep. My gut is pointing me towards Wyatt. Did you talk to Tremonti about a fishing charter like we discussed?"

Bree wagged her head. "I'm sorry, Vin. It completely slipped my mind."

"I'd like to move on this right away. Can you arrange it for tomorrow? My partner is flying in tomorrow afternoon."

"It's too late to call Wyatt's now. Let me go talk to Jack about getting up early enough in the morning to pull this off. I'll text you as soon as I have a decision for you." She stepped into the parlor.

"Good... Uh, Breeze?" sounded behind her.

The segue hinted at a longer conversation and she itched to rejoin Jack. Maybe relish a good night kiss to send her to her room floating in the same happy bubble that Vinnie's interruption had deflated.

Still, Vincente Carlucci remained a rarity in Bree's

life. A college fling had ended and against the odds had left a valued, solid friendship. Bree cared deeply for Vinnie and always would. She turned around stepping back out onto the porch. Facing him, she arched her neck to meet his dark eyes. "Yes?"

Certainly Vinnie exuded virility and confidence. He and Jack had many similar attributes that owed, perhaps, to common ethnic roots. But Bree had never entered a parallel universe gazing into Vinnie's blue eyes like she experienced each time Jack's penetrating pale gray eyes held hers.

Her overwhelming, unprecedented attraction to Jack; her admiration for all he had accomplished in his entrepreneurial career; his sweet, devoted parenting; the satisfying intellectual interplay between them; her endless supply of superlatives that fit Jack all added up to her no comparison feelings for him. There was a world of difference between fondness and borderless love.

"You know I love you, right?" he said.

"Um, sure," she said narrowing her eyes.

"I want what's best for you, OK?" he continued. "Want me to do a background check on Tremonti?"

"Are you kidding?" She hooted, amused.

His deadpan expression had her knitting her brow. "You're *serious?* Of course not."

"Just saying…"

Bree didn't like the insinuation one bit. "Don't meddle in my love life, Vin. Jack is too important to me. Please?"

"Yeah. OK," he conceded. "Just so I'm clear…how important?"

Bree smiled considering her response. "Hmm. I

guess *all* important."

He reached into his breast pocket, slipped out a pack of Marlboros, tapped out a cigarette and inserted it into the corner of his lips. Vin torched the tobacco tip with a disposable lighter and inhaled deeply. He blew smoke sideways over his shoulder and then said, "I think I always believed that we'd get together again someday. Would it make a difference if I told you I've never found anyone that I love as much as you?"

"Oh, Vin." She touched his shoulder lightly. "You'll find someone that you love beyond compare. Trust me."

He dropped his eyes. "Guess that spells it out for me."

Vinnie straightened and cast her a crooked grin. "Go check with lover boy about the fishing charter. I'll see you in the morning."

She pursed her lips and shook her head. "Gees, quit with the lover boy reference. I'll text you in a few." Bree crossed the threshold into the parlor.

Anticipating kissing Jack good night, she hurried through the front room and hallway. Bounding up the stairs she replayed the end of the conversation with Vinnie in her mind. It wasn't that she was hard-hearted or that she wholly doubted his sincerity, but she didn't take him seriously. Their relationship had been superficial at best and he had ended it years ago.

Finding Jack's door ajar, Bree tiptoed into his room. He rose from his spot on the bed propped against the headboard setting his laptop aside. Meeting her in two strides, he folded Bree in his arms. "Hey," he greeted her, his deep voice low.

She closed her eyes, circled her arms around his

back and snuggled against him, enfolded in luxurious warmth, breathing in unison with him. How lovely it would be never to leave the shelter of Jack's embrace.

Aware of the open connecting door to Gabriella's room, Bree raised her head off his shoulder and whispered, "Can you wake Ella early tomorrow? I'd love to take you out on a fishing boat."

"I'm sure she'd like that. What time?"

"Six? That's if I can arrange the charter first thing. I'll call when they open at 5:30. If a boat's not available I'll let you know so you can let her sleep?"

He nodded smiling. Jack's penetrating, passionate gaze speared her heart. The intensity of his unspoken message, I love you, had tears welling.

Jack responded with a chaste, soul stirring kiss. "Good night, darling."

Bree beamed up at him. "Good night, Jack."

She drifted down the corridor lined with guest rooms and climbed the stairs to the family wing. Bree hoped that Skye was deep asleep. The momentous first of telling the man of her dreams that she loved him and the utter joy of hearing him say the same amazing three words to her seemed too gigantic to share right then.

Skye curled on her side facing away from the door, her breathing deep and even. Bree had her wish to relish her secret a while longer.

Too tired to take a cold shower to drop the sizzling heat index mere thoughts of Jack generated, Bree sat down on her bed and lifted her cell phone off the side table.

She typed the text message, "I'll charter the boat if available at Wyatt in the morning."

Bree set the phone back on the table, stripped to

her underwear and slipped beneath the cool, lonely sheets of her maiden bed.

Chapter 17

Awake before sunrise, Bree sat on the end of her bed ready to dial Wyatt Marine. Bleary-eyed, the low battery symbol swam in the dim light—a reddish blur in the darkness.

Damn. She rose and tiptoed out of the room where her sister continued sleeping.

Downstairs, she strode to the Inn's landline on the kitchen counter. Riffling through the kitchen drawer she found a phone charger to revive her dead cell phone.

"You're up early."

Bree startled at the unexpected sound of her father's voice.

"Sorry, honey. I didn't mean to scare you. Everything OK?" Dad kissed the top of her head and took a seat, straddling the stool he pulled out from under the counter. "I hope I didn't wake you bumping around down here."

"No, I was already up. My phone died and I have to call Wyatt Marine to see if I can charter a boat for this morning."

"Don't call Wyatt. I'll call Harley for you. You know he won't charge you an arm and a leg like Wyatt will." He reached for the phone.

"Thanks, but I have to book with Wyatt."

"Why?"

"Because Jack wants to take Gabriella out on a

Wyatt boat today." Guilty with the half-truth, she averted her father's eyes.

"Why would Jack even have an opinion about charter companies? Want to tell me the real reason?"

"I don't want you involved."

"I'm your father, I'm already involved. What's going on?"

"Vinnie wants me to book the charter to get a closer look at Wyatt Marine's operation. He thinks Wyatt is responsible for that van of drugs seized on the bridge."

"That wouldn't surprise me. If you ask me the whole Wyatt family is bad news. That being said, I really don't want you anywhere near them."

"Don't worry. I'll be with Jack and Vinnie."

"And that's supposed to make me feel better? Vinnie took such good care of you the last time he got you tangled up in his business. Does Jack know what he's getting into?"

Bree had some misgivings about involving Jack in Vinnie's plan, but she couldn't see the harm in a simple boat excursion that incidentally provided cover for an FBI agent. Vinnie didn't expect her or Jack to do anything but enjoy the day.

"Vinnie's on his own with the investigation. We won't be affected at all," she assured him.

Confident in her reasoning, Bree dialed Wyatt Marine as she paced in front of the coffee pot anticipating her first sip of the heavenly, aromatic brew.

"Crap." Bree set the portable phone into the charger station. "I got a recorded message that they're not running charters for the next two weeks."

"That's interesting. Guess you'll call Harley after

all," he said. "Besides, nothing gets by him on the Banks. Vinnie can pick his brain. Maybe come at Wyatt indirectly."

"But, you can't tell Harley about the investigation."

"I won't. I don't need to...you know Harley. Once he starts talking you can't stop him."

"Thanks. I guess it's worth a try. Could you tell him we only need the charter for a couple of hours?"

"Sure. I haven't seen Harley in a few weeks. He was up north spending some time with his boys. Mind if I tag along?"

"Not at all. I'd love for you to come."

"Sign me up, too." Skye breezed into the room and put the tea kettle on the stove.

Bree chuckled, accustomed to her family's habit of eavesdropping.

"I've been meaning to stop by Harley's," Skye said. "He wants me to paint some gifts for his daughters in law for Christmas."

****

A half hour later beneath a sunrise sky streaked blood red and tangerine orange, Jack, Bree, Gabriella, Mike, Skye and Vinnie piled into the Inn's van. The aroma of fresh brewed coffee from four travel mugs filled the interior. The sun just breached the horizon as Mike drove over the Washington Baum Bridge. Bree snuggled next to Jack as he circled his arm around her shoulders. She closed her eyes and melted into his warmth. Last night she worried that their rocket-fast romance might amount to nothing more than a beach fling. Would Jack regret that he said he loved her? Did those three words carry the same meaning for him: life changing, permanent...forever?

He beamed at her, his smoldering gaze banishing doubt. She thought she understood Jack's wordless message as his eyes held hers. Fear abated as he seemed to express that he was hers—destined to walk into the Inn on a fluke, the embodiment of prayers answered.

"Hey, princess," Vinnie craned his neck around the headrest of the passenger seat, and smiled at Ella. "Are you gonna catch the biggest fish?"

She wagged her head vigorously. "Ew, no. I don't want to catch any fish."

"You sound just like Bree and Skye," Mike said. "Every time Harley and I took the girls and his sons out on the boat to catch some fish we wound up watching the dolphins instead."

Bree shot a playful smile at Skye. "Those boys were so mad at us. They refused to let us on their boats for years. They would only let Summer go with them. She usually caught more fish than the boys did combined."

"I believe that. Summer has ba—" Vinnie bit back the off-color remark and substituted, "Summer is one tough cookie."

Mike parked in the marina's lot and the passengers poured out of the van onto the gravel. Bree spied Harley, his bear-like silhouette haloed by the sun, standing next to a sleek sport-fishing cabin cruiser, *No Regrets* painted in forest green on its stern. Sidling up to Harley, Dad made the introductions. Harley shook the men's hands, winked at Ella who leaned shyly against Jack's side and doled out warm hugs to Bree and Skye.

Harley cupped Skye's elbows and held her at arm's length. "I've been meaning to tell you, darlin'. A man was in my office about a month ago. Saw the mermaid and offered me five thousand dollars on the spot."

"You have a mermaid in your office?" Ella said, her eyes wide.

"Oh no, honey." Skye crouched next to her. "It's not a real mermaid, just a painting of one."

"*Just* a painting?" Harley's voice boomed. "It is the most beautiful painting of a mermaid you'll ever see. After our boat ride I can show it to you if you want."

"Yes." Ella grinned. Apparently comfortable with the burly man, she linked hands with Harley allowing him to help her board the boat.

"Harley commissioned Skye to paint his wife Hannah's face on the mermaid's body. It was the last Christmas gift he gave Hannah before she died of cancer," Bree informed Jack.

"Nice boat you got here, Harley," Vinnie declared. Striding up and down the dock he surveyed the vessel. "What's she got? Twin Caterpillar Diesel Engines?"

"Good call," Harley said, nodding.

"Does he always wear his shirts two sizes too small?" Jack quipped to Mike who responded with a snigger.

Bree bit back a laugh at the probably jealousy-fueled remark and watched Vinnie closely.

"She's a true Carolina-style fishing boat, the Cadillac of the Ocean," Vinnie said.

Was she the only one who noticed that his focus was narrowed on the coastal surroundings, not on Harley's boat at all?

"I'm impressed. You know your marine vessels, young man."

"I've watched *Wicked Tuna*."

Harley and Mike hooted a laugh.

Jack snorted. "Yeah and I've watched *Grey's Anatomy*. Doesn't make me a surgeon."

Vinnie reacted to Jack's aside. He glared at Jack who glared back. Threat shimmered in the air. Their faces froze as if battle ready and the two men deadlocked eyes for several alarming seconds before Vinnie seemed to shake the whole thing off. "Right, Jack," he said casually. "Just making conversation."

Jack wouldn't be bested by Vinnie in the equanimity war. "Sure. No offense meant."

"No problem," Vinnie tossed out, sweeping past Jack. Gauging the rocking motion of the boat moored at the dock he leapt aboard nimbly; surprisingly light on his huge feet. He climbed up to the flybridge, a seaman in the crow's nest position.

The Captain and a crew member boarded and took the helm. Anchors away, the engines fired and *No Regrets* sailed gracefully out of the slip.

"I just got a bottle of the latest shipwreck series rum from the distillery. It adds a nice flavor to a cup of coffee. Can I interest anyone in a cup?" Harley offered as they passed under the Bonner Bridge.

Harley, and Mike disappeared below deck to the galley to grab the spiked coffee and conversation.

Skye and Gabriella sat on the cushioned bench in the bow cockpit; their gazes scanning the waves hoping for a dolphin sighting.

Bree and Jack settled into the mezzanine fishing chairs ignoring the rods, swinging the swivel chairs to face each other.

"Not interested in some rum-laced coffee?"

"You're intoxicating enough." He wiggled his

eyebrows.

"Nice line." Bree smiled as Jack took her hand. "How 'bout some fishing?"

"Nah. I'd rather look at you." His face transformed with his smile.

Bree beamed back at him, enthralled, elated.

"This is some boat," he said. "What's Harley's story?"

"What do you mean?"

"A ship this size with a crew to sail it for you. He doesn't fit with my expectation of a fisherman."

"You're right. He's actually more business man than fisherman. Ever see the triple H van line trucks?"

"Of course, who hasn't? I used HHH when we moved into the condo."

"Harley Hannah Hauling."

"Interesting. I never realized the letters were initials."

"Hannah was born and raised on the Banks. They met while he was on vacation and their whirlwind love story began. He proposed at the end of his two week stay here."

Bree's heart leapt at the similarity between Hannah's and her romantic circumstances. "After the wedding, Harley renamed his company and took his bride home. She tried to live in Atlanta where the company was based but missed home too much. Harley would do anything for Hannah so he moved with her back to her beloved Banks, bought a plane and commuted from Manteo to Atlanta on Sunday evenings and back every Friday night. He bought the fishing fleet and began running charters shortly after his second son was born, mostly for fun. But he has the knack for business and it was successful early on. They lived their fairytale. He's virtually lost since she passed. The boys, well, they're men now, have taken over HHH. They keep pressuring him to move back to Atlanta, but he won't leave. He says he feels Hannah's presence in the morning when he walks the beach. This boat was originally christened *Triple H.* After Hannah died he renamed her *No Regrets.*"

Jack made no comment. She couldn't read his thoughts and insecurity swelled within her. "How about you? You said you loved me. Any regrets?"

"Regrets? No. More like I'm in shock."

She frowned, offended that he could describe loving her in such negative terms.

He squeezed her hand to prevent her from yanking it out of his grasp. His eyes sparked with the wry twist of his lips. "Don't pull away, Bree."

Jack brought her hand to his lips and gently kissed her knuckles one by one.

Involuntarily, Bree closed her eyes, softening... melting. How easily he swayed her.

Both his hands encapsulated hers, intensifying her deep thrall. "What I meant is that I'm shocked at how fast my feelings for you have grown. I hadn't planned on telling you how I feel. I just blurted it out. But I always say what I mean. I love you, Bree. I've only said that to one other woman in my life. And I dated Sophia for months before I ever told her I loved her. This impulsiveness is new to me. I like it." He raised her hand again and kissed her palm. "Do you ask because you have regrets?"

Bree wagged her head. "None. I thought it was a dream when I woke up this morning." She gazed into his soft dove-colored eyes and smiled. "But then you put your arm around me in the van, and I knew it was real. I've never felt this way about anyone."

"Vinnie didn't make your heart flutter?"

She huffed a laugh. "Nope. Maybe I wished that he did once. But I didn't want to settle. I waited for true love."

"Are you saying that I'm your true love?" he teased.

"Maybe..." Bree arched her back and leaned forward. She brushed a kiss on his lips. "You're definitely worth waiting for."

"Daddy, Daddy look at this!" came Ella's gleeful voice from below.

Ella waved a piece of paper overhead and then began climbing the ladder. Bree scooted out of her chair, reached down and accepted the paper Ella held up while she perched on the middle rung.

Jack sidled up behind Bree and viewed the drawing of four dolphins dancing in the waves depicted on the page—Skye's touch in the sketch evident to Bree.

"I did most of it myself. Skye helped," Ella chattered. "Skye said I could be an artist just like her."

"This is really good, sweetheart." He hung onto the rails, leaned down and planted a kiss on Ella's pink cheek. "Can you sign it for me like Skye signs her paintings? I want to frame it and hang it in my office."

Ella grinned up at her father basking in the praise. "Did you see the dolphins following the boat? Skye said if you sit really quiet and just whisper their names they will hear you and come. We sat so quiet and Skye whispered Charlie, Buddy and then I whispered their names, too, and they came!

"That's Charlie." She pointed to the largest dolphin. "And that's Buddy right next to him. There's Marigold out in the waves. See the little one next to her?"

Jack followed her tracing the page with a finger. "That's her baby Petunia. Skye said Marigold won't come near the boat, she has to protect Petunia."

She snatched the paper out of Jack's hand. "I have to get back to Skye. I'll sign my name for you, Daddy." Rising up on her tip-toes, she kissed Jack's cheek.

Jack watched her descend the ladder and hop down to the lower deck.

"Your sister certainly has a way with children," he said.

"Skye's a very special soul."

"It's probably harmless that Gabriella believes Skye can summon dolphins at will, right Doc?"

"You'll have to get to know my sister better before you doubt her."

Jack rounded his eyes. "Wait. You don't believe that Skye talks to the dolphins, do you?"

Mike and Harley made a commotion emerging from the galley. Judging from their jovial expressions, the coffee cups they toted held a generous amount of rum.

"Settle an argument for us. Who has the best pitching this year? The Yankees or the Red Sox?" Harley said.

"Cubs. Hands down," Jack piped up.

"Yankees," came Vinnie's unwelcome opinion from the upper deck.

"Figures," Jack muttered.

Deep in thought, Bree sat back in her chair and

listened with half an ear to the men's banter. The wind whipped her hair off her forehead and water droplets sprinkled her as the hull slapped the waves. Before this relationship went any further she would have to reveal to Jack that The Legend isn't a legend. She had never become entangled enough with a man before to have to explain her family history. With Jack everything was different. She couldn't move on without his knowing everything.

Chapter 18

"Hey, Breeze!" Vinnie's booming baritone blasted from above Bree's head.

Shading her eyes with her hand she gazed up in his direction. He hung over the railing with binoculars in his left hand, waving "come here" at her with furious sweeps of his right arm. Dark glasses obscured his eyes but his tensed jaw and the unbroken straight line of his lips told her he was serious about the reason he beckoned.

Without consulting Jack in word or gesture, she scooted out of the swivel chair and climbed the ladder to join Vinnie on the flybridge. She thought she felt Jack's disapproving gaze boring into her back as she climbed each rung.

Vinnie's musky cologne overpowered the briny scented breeze. "What do you need, Vin?"

"Let's make like you're showing me the controls over here?" He gestured to the console with a snap of his head, but his eyes held hers. "If you can, check out the cove at approximately two o'clock. Try naked eye first."

The drag on Jack's spinning reel screamed, drawing Bree's attention to the action on the deck below. She leaned over the railing, delighted with Jack's athletic performance; man versus fish.

"Whoa!" Jack gripped the nodding pole, angling

back against the opposition of his catch. "Gabriella, come see," he called.

Now he surged to his feet as he evenly reeled in the line, all breath robbing tensed muscles and glistening tanned skin, his dark hair whipping in the wind, unruly and sexy. Ella zipped to the stern and clambered up the ladder. At Jack's elbow she voiced encouragement. "Go Daddy! You can do it."

The fish breached, silver glints sparkling in the wake of the vessel. Unrelenting, Jack planted his feet widely on the deck and kept reeling in the line.

"Wait." Ella touched Jack's bulging bicep. "You're going to let him go, right, Daddy?"

"Yep. Hey, Harley?" he shouted.

"Yo," came the response.

"If I bring this fish close to the side, can you help free it?"

"You crazy, man?" Harley boomed. "That's prime Carolina tuna on the end of that line."

Jack's hearty laugh floated on the wind. "Gotta make my girl happy."

Bree smiled, mesmerized and increasingly impressed with Jack's tenderness with Ella.

"Hey!" came Vinnie's basso voice behind her.

She jolted and turned towards him, irritated with the interruption. *"What?"*

"Hurry up and check out that cove. We're almost out of range. But try not to be too obvious."

"Yeah, OK." Pivoting towards the stern again as if watching Jack and Harley "un-catch" the fish, Bree squinted and focused shoreward. "Can't see details in the cove. Looks like a boat moored leeward," she tossed out over her shoulder.

"Here." Vinnie suspended the binoculars in front of her face. "Use these. Make it quick."

Still irritated by his brusqueness, Bree raised the binoculars to her eyes and adjusted her focus on the craft anchored in the cove. Harley had cut the engine on *No Regrets* to help Jack deal with the mammoth snagged tuna. The boat bobbed on swells fragmenting Bree's line of sight. She made out a few letters painted on the transom of the boat in the cove partially obscured by the curve of land. "I can make out an O an F and an I in sequence. The boat name. Not much else."

About to lower the binoculars, Bree was surrounded by Vinnie's looming brawn. His arms encircled her shoulders and he wrapped his hands around hers pressing the binoculars into her eye sockets. The scope wiggled against her face as he loosed one hand and fiddled with buttons atop the binoculars. The view zoomed in as if the boat were a few feet away. The lettering on the transom was crisp and clear: OFISH 2. "Oh," she said. "That's one of the *Gofish* boats. They're Wyatt cruisers."

"Thought so," he rumbled. He was so close to her that his voice created vibrations against Bree's back. He exerted slight pressure on a button atop the binoculars. "You're recording. Pan the area once and then let's turn away and mess with buttons on the console up here. Don't know who's watching."

Bree positioned the viewfinder to start with the rocky outcrop at one side of the mouth of the cove and moved the digital binoculars in a slow arc left to right. At the median, she could see the rear deck of the boat clearly. Her breath caught in her throat.

"Oh my God." Randy Wyatt, gawked at her, his

yellow-toothed leer making her skin crawl.

Forcibly she shook Vinnie's hands away so she could lower the binoculars.

"What?" Vinnie spun her to face him, took the binoculars out of her hands, pushed the button to stop recording, and draped the strap over his head.

"So creepy." She leaned against the railing catching her breath. "Randy Wyatt was staring straight back at me looking through binoculars. I could actually see every rotten tooth."

Bree shook off the vision waggling her shoulders. "Ugh."

Vinnie leaned towards Bree grasping a handhold on either side of the railing behind her, wedging her between his arms. Leaning close, he said, "Thanks for confirming my target."

"Aren't you worried he'll be suspicious that the FBI is on to him? He obviously knows he's being watched."

"I can't believe he'd see you as a threat. I wouldn't have involved you otherwise." Vinnie pushed away from the rail and planted his feet on the deck in front of her as Harley gunned the engine. "And my guess is he didn't notice me or anybody else on this boat. Not when he can ogle pretty Breeze."

He tipped a finger under her chin and grinned. "You couldn't have done better. Really worked out that Harley's charter was all that was available. I'm solid on the investigation now. Thanks, Breeze."

Vinnie swept her into a hug.

"Um…" Disengaging, Bree stood upright poised to descend the ladder. "Well… you take it from here, Vin. I'm officially out of the spy game."

Bree zipped down the ladder and nimbly hopped onto the mezzanine deck. When she turned towards the stern, she found Skye and Jack beaming judgmental vibes up at her.

"Hey," she said, uncertain at what she interpreted as their disapproval. "Amazing catch, Jack."

"Thanks." His tone was offhand and impersonal as he grabbed a rung of the ladder.

Skye drifted back to the seating on the bow presumably to entertain Ella. Reaching Bree's level, Jack stowed his fishing pole and then repositioned in a swivel chair.

"Done with fishing?" Bree sat next to him.

"Yeah. Just going to enjoy the view for now."

She wasn't positive about what she might have done to deserve the cold shoulder, although she didn't rule out his now seeing through to the underlying reason she had arranged the fishing expedition.

Maybe she should have confided in Jack about Vinnie's request for the marine surveillance. The specter of Randy Wyatt staring back at her through binoculars stayed with her; sinister and somehow threatening. Was he involved in the crimes Vinnie was investigating?

Probably. Without meaning to, Bree was complicit with Vinnie and might have put them all in danger. She would hear no end of this from Skye. And she'd have to admit her involvement, albeit with innocent intentions, and a great deal more to Jack for their relationship to thrive.

Bree shivered. She couldn't envision a future without Jack and Ella. It didn't matter that a short while ago she didn't know that Jack existed—except perhaps in her far flung fantasies. Her soul recognized its mate and she wouldn't let her guilt or his snit ruin destiny.

****

Back home, Bree almost lost the chance to smooth things over with Jack. As soon as Dad braked in the van's parking place, Jack bolted out of his seat, Ella in tow. On a bead toward the building, he seemed intent on avoiding her.

"Jack! Hold up."

He halted and pivoted slowly, the expression on his face, closed—unreadable.

Skye apparently didn't need supernatural ability to interpret the situation, however. She zipped past Bree and shepherded Ella, taking the little girl's hand. "Let's check out the beach," she suggested.

Baby duck Ella followed mama Skye to the next adventure.

Bree caught up with Jack and touched his shoulder gently. "Are you mad at me?"

"No." He turned away from her and paced forward.

"Whoa," she said in motion. She scooted in front of him and blocked his progress. "Obviously you are. Do I need to apologize? Talk to me, Jack."

"I don't want your apologies. I have no one to blame but myself." He shouldered past her and strode forward.

With no ground left to hold, Bree stood helplessly as he stalked out of site behind the building.

Mike sidled up beside her. "You could cut through the parlor and kitchen. Head him off at the deck."

Bree smiled at his wink and then broke into a run. Blasting out onto the deck she sighted her quarry. She caught Jack's eye and beckoned him with a wave of her hand.

Apparently resigned to confrontation, he trudged through the sand, mounted the wooden steps and joined her on the deck.

"Sit?" She pointed toward the deck chairs.

"If you say so."

Bree took the lead. "I'm sorry that I involved you with Vinnie. Truly, I don't believe that there's any harm done."

His eyes darkened, a twister brewing in storm cloud gray eyes. "What do you mean involved *me* with him? I'm pissed that *you're* involved with that guy."

He stared seaward, his jaw clenched. "For me, love is exclusive. I'm sorry that I assumed you'd believe the same thing."

Bree frowned. "Of course I believe that. What does that have to do with this? I'm sorry because I shouldn't have let him convince me to help him investigate charter companies."

"Wait. What?" He jolted out of the chair, which scraped harshly on the floorboards with his weight shift. "You set up a ruse with him? And dragged us into it? Are you kidding me?"

Guilt pinched. "No, no. It was a simple request to take him along so he could look around the coast…and maybe poke around the charter operation we used." She sighed and prayed she hadn't inadvertently betrayed Jack's trust in her judgment.

Jack wagged his head. "Wow." Leaning forward he barricaded her, one hand on each armrest of the Adirondack chair. Ominously close, his voice registered as a shout. "Your feelings for him obviously run deep. I'm done being a victim. And I sure as hell won't let my daughter be victimized."

He shoved the chair away roughly sliding Bree backward a few inches and stomped into the building leaving Bree teary-eyed and deflated. Taking ragged breaths, she watched Skye and Ella advance towards her.

****

As if the cards had purposefully stacked against him, Jack almost crashed into Vinnie as he marched into the kitchen. In no mood to deal with the guy's cocksure manner, he swerved around him heading towards the stairs.

"Something eating you, Jack?"

Exasperated, Jack couldn't resist confrontation. He whirled on the G-man and spit out, "Yeah. You could say that."

An intense desire to jab the smirk right off Vinnie's face flooded him. But he stayed put in the faceoff, fuming inside. How he'd worked up to this irrational jealousy mystified him while at the same time left him powerless to feel differently.

Vinnie spared him from further comment by hitting the nail on the head. "You don't like me at all. Right?"

Jack glared at him. "Understatement."

"I take it you think that Breeze is your woman. And I'm trespassing. Have I got that right?"

He narrowed his eyes shooting a salvo of utter disdain at Vinnie. "Maybe. Among other things."

With his palms out-stretched Vinnie signaled a truce. "Look. I'll admit I flat out love that girl. We go back. But...she has wanted nothing to do with *anything* beyond friendship with me for *years.*"

He raised his right hand. "Hand to God, Jack. She's

in love with you. And whether you believe it or not, I accept that."

Momentarily appeased, thoughts of Bree working with Vinnie behind his back stoked his anger again. "How is it that the two of you conspired to work together on *your* investigation and involved me and my daughter without my knowledge?"

Vinnie twisted his lips. "Oh. Yeah. Well I kind of took advantage of the friendship a little there, pal."

"Don't pal me. Do I have to worry about Gabriella's safety?"

He did a double take. "What? No. I'd never put innocents in harm's way. Bree never would have agreed otherwise no matter how hard I pushed the friendship factor. If your nose is out of joint with her because of that you're *way* out of line."

Jack recognized the ring of truth. "Good...thanks. For setting me straight."

Remorse spurred him forward to seek out Bree and apologize for his outburst. Halfway across the kitchen he was met with Gabriella and Skye bursting through the sliding door, bogged down with net bags of seashells.

"Come on, Daddy," Gabriella chattered. "We're going upstairs to wash the sand off these shells and put them on my window seat."

Stroking her damp hair, Jack shifted his priorities. He'd find Bree and beg her forgiveness later. "Sure. Let's go."

Chapter 19

Bree knotted her fists and pressed her knuckles into the corners of her eyes to stem the tears. Victim? How had she victimized Jack? Although she hadn't informed him of Vinnie's behind the scenes request, she never would have predicted Jack's furious reaction. Was she wrong about him? He was completely wrong about her if he believed she would ever endanger a child. Furious with herself for letting her emotions run wild she rose from the deck chair and slapped her hand against the weathered railing. She relished the physical sting that banished earlier tears and snapped her back to the "real" world. How stupid to believe that she could experience true love in less than a week?

She calculated the sum total of her knowledge of Jack aside from his irresistible physicality. He liked the same pizza; he was a great father; his marriage was disintegrating before tragedy ended it; he only recently emerged from the nightmare of his daughter's PTSD and he was a good kisser. An unforgettable kisser.

Bree slapped the railing again, her insides twisting with equal parts longing and exasperation. She had to rethink her recent fantasizing. How could she build a life with Jack on such a shaky foundation?

A gust of wind flung her hair around her face. She snapped a scrunchie off of her wrist, captured her wayward tresses between two hands and twisted the elastic around her mane, fashioning a loose bun atop her head.

"You know how much I like your hair up like that." Bree jolted at Vinnie's gentle touch on the nape of her neck.

Reflexively she swatted his hand away as she spun around and squinted up at his handsome face. "You! I could kill you right now." She balled her hands at her side.

"Sweetheart, it's not wise to make death threats to an FBI agent."

His belly laughing made her even angrier. She punched his arm taking out her frustration with Jack on him. Quite satisfying emotionally, but physically—not so much.

"Ouch!" A searing pain shot from her fist to her apparently still injured shoulder. "Shit." She kneaded the painful scar.

"Are you OK?" Vinnie extended his hand towards her shoulder as if to comfort her.

Even though she believed that his concern was genuine, she rejected his sentiment and shoved his hand away from her. "I'm fine. And don't give me that puppy dog look. I'm really mad at you."

"Why? What did I do?" Scowling, he slid his sunglasses up on top of his head.

Bree closed her eyes, heaved a sigh and wagged her head realizing how wrong she was to direct her anger at anyone else but Jack.

She faced Vinnie squarely. "Nothing. You really didn't do anything. I'm sorry I blamed you. I'm royally pissed and you just stepped right into the bull's-eye."

"Fire away, lady if it makes you feel better. I take it

things aren't going well with lover boy."

Before she could sidestep, he swept her into a bear hug, crushing her against his chest.

Bree wrenched away with a rapid twist of her torso. "I asked you to stop calling him that," she spat out. "And stop gloating."

"I'm not gloating. You have to know by now that I only want what's best for you. Do I think that I'm the best man for you? Damned straight I do. But you and I, pretty lady haven't seen eye to eye on that subject for years. So... I'm trying my hardest to respect your feelings. But when I see some jerk hurting you..."

She cut him off, "He is *not* a jerk."

"Fine. When I see some great guy hurting you, I can't help it. I want to smash his face in."

Bree almost giggled at his machismo, but caught herself. The last thing she wanted was a fistfight between these two alphas.

"I'm sorry. Tell me what did the jer...what did Jack do?"

"Huh," she huffed considering his obvious lack of remorse. "*Jack* is mad at me for taking his daughter on your boat ride. I guess he has every right to be angry. I didn't consult him before involving him and Ella in your investigation."

Pensively she rubbed her shoulder. "Maybe I shouldn't have been so quick to agree to helping you, Vin. Not the best judgment call on my part."

"Don't start doubting yourself. You're the most level headed person I know. Not to mention the smartest." He held his arms out, open-palmed. "What matters is nothing bad happened. Nothing bad will ever happen on my watch. I would never put a child at risk.

Beautiful women …maybe. But not kids."

He waggled his eyebrows. Bree burst out laughing.

"And for the record," he added. "I straightened him out just now."

His statement had Bree swallowing laughter. "Wait…what?" She clasped his arm. "Tell me *exactly* what you said to him about me."

Gifting her with a crooked grin, he said, "I can't remember exactly. But it was nice," he teased.

"Seriously, Vin…" she squeezed his elbow.

"Man…" He rubbed his elbow feigning injury. "No need to torture it out of me."

Bree spun on her heel, traversed the deck and bounded down the steps. It was bad enough that Jack's jealousy, or whatever it was, had him facing off with her. But Vinnie's interference and trampling on her fledgling romance… perhaps with his own ulterior motives? She had had enough.

From behind her came thudding footsteps and the winded plea, "Hold up, princess. No need to stomp off. I'm on your side."

Reluctantly she stopped and waited for him to catch up with her.

"Listen," he said. "I basically told Jack that as much as I don't want to, I accept that you choose him."

She narrowed her eyes. "Vinnie, I resent your involvement in my personal life. You are *really* putting a strain on our friendship."

"Hey, I'll back off from now on. That's more or less what I said to him anyway. *Plus,* I convinced him that no endangerment was involved with the boat charter."

"All right…"

"He thanked me for setting him straight. Hand to God."

Vinnie raised his right hand and struck an eagle scout-like pose. "Forgiven?"

She huffed a sigh and gave him a thin smile. "I guess. But stop messing with him."

"Understood. Come on. Let's go for a walk. You've never shown me your magical beach that you always talk about."

As she turned into the stiff wind, the scrunchie in Bree's hair let loose and sailed into a rolling landing on the sand. Vinnie bent down to retrieve it as a ghost crab darted, and tried to drag it into his hole.

"No you don't, little guy." He snatched the hair holder and shook off the sand. The crab seemed to glare, his black eye-dots atop antennae angled up at the tall man, before he disappeared beneath the sand.

"Nasty little buggers." Vinnie sidestepped another crab that popped up in front of his huge feet.

"They won't bother you." Bree accepted the hair holder and wrapped it around her wrist.

She paced in silence along the water's edge sensing that Vinnie had more to impart to her.

When he didn't volunteer she probed, "What's up? I can tell there's something swirling around in that brain of yours."

"You psychiatrists are always analyzing."

"You FBI agents are always dodging questions."

"Touché. I'm moving out when we get back to the Inn."

"Why? Don't tell me it has to do with me and Jack. You enjoy stirring people up way too much for me to believe that."

"Yeah well, touché again. But lover boy isn't the reason. The case will finish tonight."

"Really?" She came to a halt and gazed up at his face. "I don't understand. Only a few hours ago you were cruising the Sound beginning your investigation. Now all of a sudden you have all the answers?"

"My partner, Gerry and a team are here, too. We've been on the island for over a month. It's been so long since I've seen you, I stopped by the Inn, when I heard you were home helping out your parents. I never thought they would invite me to stay. After the shooting, I thought they would never want to see me again."

"You could have rejected the invitation."

"Sure. But they were so gracious. I didn't want to insult them and it was good to see everyone again...especially in a different place other than a college campus...or a hospital room. Your family is so welcoming. Well, most of them are. For such a free spirit, Skye can sure hold a grudge."

"You don't understand her. It's not a grudge exactly. She remembers the pain. Acutely. It's a triplets thing. Maybe it's impossible to understand how special our...relationship is."

Although her history with Vinnie included dating him, and she considered Vinnie her closest male friend now, Bree had never shared the sisters' connection to The Legend or Skye's special powers with him.

Up until recently, Bree had never seen the need to reveal that intimate information to anyone. She was on the verge of telling Jack the truth before he acted like an ass.

"At least Summer doesn't seem to hold the

shooting against me anymore."

Bree didn't like that gleam in Vinnie's eye. "Careful, Vin. I won't let my sister be one of your flings."

He thumped his fist against his breastbone and doubled over as if stabbed in the heart. "That hurt."

"Yeah, right. Consider yourself forewarned."

Bree resumed strolling along the beach. Vinnie fell into step beside her. She picked up the thread of conversation about the conclusion of his investigation. "After we spotted his boat in the cove, did you confirm that Randy is involved in your case?"

"We have a lead that something big is going down tonight. And yes, Randy is deep in this."

"Where did the lead come from?"

"We have an undercover agent crewing one of the Wyatt boats. It's taken us months to infiltrate the operation. We thought it had paid off the other night. We had surveillance on the van and a two-vehicle tail in progress. The assumption was that the van was headed to the mainland distribution source, and then up the Eastern Seaboard. But, damn it, the driver spotted us and rabbited."

"I read all about it in the paper. Honestly, I was shocked to read that drugs were such a problem here. I guess growing up I was pretty sheltered. Thought we were remote enough to be immune to big city problems."

"No place is safe. Trust me, illegal drugs are epidemic. Losing over seven million in product puts Randy in deep shit. He's unraveling and making stupid mistakes."

"That's right. Seven million. They mentioned the

sum in the article," Bree said. "Are you sure you have the right suspect? Randy and his family live in an oversized shack by the Sound."

"Don't be fooled by appearances. Randy is the middleman in the operation. Informants claim there's an ax over his head. He needs to replace the confiscated load tonight or he might wind up as shark chum."

Bree shivered at the prospect. "So what exactly happens tonight?"

Vinnie came to a standstill. Bree stopped walking, too. The waves gently rolled towards her propelling cool water against her ankles and then suctioning away on the ebb, sinking her feet in the sand. He circled an arm around her shoulder. "I think I've told you too much already. Maybe that's because I miss discussing cases with you. I love the way you can get inside people's heads."

"I don't think you need much help getting inside Randy's head. From what I remember about him there's not much there."

He chortled, a companionable rumble against her side. After checking a glimpse at his watch he said, "Let's turn around. I have to shove off soon."

Something was off in the tone of his voice and she angled her head to appraise his face. "Are you OK? You look tired."

"I'm good. Just have a lot of balls in the air right now. I don't like being away from Tricia so long."

"How is your sister?"

"She's coming along. Who knew that Barry would turn into such a shmuck and run off with his secretary? What a cliché, right?"

"How are the kids doing?"

"My mom and pop have helped out. Barry Jr. has acted out a lot and is hard to handle. But I try to get there to pitch in every weekend. I'm long overdue."

"You really are a good man under all that macho. Send your parents my love, and tell Tricia if she needs anything I'm just a phone call away.

"Thanks. You're the best, Breeze. I hope Jack knows how lucky he is." He planted a soft kiss on the top of her head.

He paused at the foot of the stairs, looking at the ocean, a soft expression on his face. "There really is something about this place that draws me. As soon as I have free time, I think I'll bring Trisha and the kids here."

"You know you're always welcome."

"Thanks. Now let's see if I can snag a few cookies to take back with me to the hotel."

Bree toed off her sandals and minced across the hot sand towards the water spigot, Vinnie in her wake.

"Be careful tonight, Vin," she said relinquishing her spot under the foot bath to him. "Can you please send a text to let me know you're safe?"

"See? My girl still cares about me." He gave her a wink and then followed Bree into the kitchen.

Chapter 20

Once JET Industries became a *Forbes* list darling, Jack publicly became known as the quintessential self-made, "genius" entrepreneur. His vision in tech design, talent selection, non-conformist management style and formulating the company's leaps ahead of the competition strategy all added up to genius. Even more unusual and extremely rare? He wasn't just popular with underlings; he was beloved. Seated on the edge of the bed, Jack thumbed through the business magazine's pages after scanning the article about JET that basically kept his sainted business reputation intact.

In front of Jack, Gabriella sat back on her haunches and fussed with the freshly washed seashell collection she had assembled on the cushions of the window seat, her small rounded back to him. Observing her unaware emphasized her vulnerability and fragile innocence. He had screwed up royally with his little girl since Sophia's fatal accident. The memory of Gabriella's unresponsiveness haunted him. He still didn't understand the serendipity that brought him here and resulted in her almost miraculous normalcy. He fully understood, however, that he had had nothing to do with Gabriella's recovery and most likely everything to do with her earlier state.

He tossed the magazine aside as thoughts of his most recent screw up with Bree came to mind. The last attribute Jack would use to describe himself was genius unless he was being very sarcastic. Jack didn't look forward to the new round of groveling he'd have with Bree. But there was no doubt he'd engage. The prospect of losing Bree now was just as terrible as the loss he had suffered with Gabriella until they checked into this place. Everything about this vacation seemed too marvelous to last. But maybe... He had to believe that his daughter and the woman he loved would stay with him.

Compelled to stand and stretch his legs, Jack drifted near Gabriella and looked out through the bay window at the sandy panorama topped by ocean blue. Movement to his right caught his eye. Bree and that pain in the ass, Vinnie, strolled along the beach and stopped, apparently conversing. Jealousy involuntarily stabbed him again. He forced himself to release distrust and accept that there was nothing but friendship between Bree and Vinnie. He finally believed that no matter what the pain in the ass wanted, Bree wanted nothing but friendship with the overbearing man. Unbelievably, she wanted Jack's love.

Since Bree was obviously occupied, there was no rush to seek her out and beg forgiveness for his outburst. "Hey," he said, draping an arm around Gabriella's warm little body. "What are you doing with these seashells?"

"Um..." She fingered a delicate, cone shaped shell. "I just like to touch the shells we found."

She lifted the shell up until it almost touched the bridge of her nose and scrutinized it as she rotated the cone. "Isn't it pretty? Like art. That's what Skye says. She says that nature makes the best art."

Gabriella nestled the tiny specimen back onto the seat cushion.

"You really love Skye, don't you?"

"Oh *yes*." She examined a smooth shell fragment, surely scooped up because of its striking purple-hued striations. "Skye is *magic*. She knows all the names of the sea animals and can talk with them whenever she wants."

"That's great," Jack said, appreciating his daughter's imagination. "Kind of like Doctor Doolittle, right?"

Her brow furrowed. "Uh..."

"Sort of," came her conclusion. "I love Bree, too...a lot. Even though she's not magic."

I don't know about that. She's cast a spell on me.

"You know, I've thought a lot about how things have changed for you...and me, since we came here. Do you feel like things have changed?"

"Sure," she said, casual, as if her absolute transformation was ordinary, easy. No reason for her father to have rejected one psychiatric opinion after another the past six months. She only needed some ocean air? Or maybe she only needed Bree, the right psychiatrist. The right everything.

"Honey, do you think you can talk to me about how you felt when Momma died?" He held his breath, fearful that he pushed her too far.

Without hesitation her head bobbed up and down. And thankfully, she coupled the body language with, "Yes."

"What do you remember about the accident?" he probed.

"I was watching Frozen on the screen. And I had

191

my headphones on."

"OK." That killed Jack's long-held assumption that Gabriella had unwittingly distracted her mother and harbored guilt about possibly causing the accident. Or that Sophia had complained about him to their daughter, her attention on the backseat instead of on the red light at the intersection.

"But I could still hear Mommy yelling on her phone."

Jack's stomach sunk at the memory of the vitriol-filled voicemail message that comprised Sophia's last words to him.

"Was she talking on the Bluetooth speaker in the car?"

She wagged her head, no.

"Did you just hear yelling?" he sincerely hoped. "Or what Mommy said?"

Tears welled in the doe eyes she trained on him. Jack inhaled sharply at the pain that stabbed deep within his chest, helplessly witnessing her suffering. Instinctively he embraced her. "It's all right, baby. You don't have to talk about it anymore if it bothers you."

Sobs wracked her body, quaking within his arms. Was it a critical and necessary catharsis? Or was he unwittingly torturing her? Maybe making things worse? God forbid, maybe casting her into silence again?

He had to stop this. It didn't matter if he ever knew the whole truth about Sophia's last minutes or Gabriella's role, if any, in the accident. He had to cherish his daughter and make certain that from now on he never contributed one iota to her anguish.

"Shh," he soothed. "You're OK, my darling. I'm here. I'll always be here." He rubbed soft circles on her back as the trembling diminished and then stilled.

"You know what? I feel like some fresh air. How about you?" he tossed out when she seemed fully composed.

She raised her head and gazed directly at him, tears lingering in the corners of her eyes and dewy streaks down her face. Sniffling, she nodded.

Jack sprang up and offered his hand to her, hoisting Gabriella up to her feet when she accepted the handhold. He dashed to the bedside table and tugged two tissues out of the box and passed them to her. She blew her nose, discarded the tissues in the waste basket and then glanced at him expectantly.

"Want to go walk along the beach for a while?" he suggested in response to her unspoken question.

"Yes. Can I bring a net bag for shells?"

"Sure. Where is it?"

"I'll get it," she said breathlessly, already on a bead to her room.

She emerged through the connecting door toting the bag and trailed Jack to the hall door. He offered her his hand and was delighted when she clamped on, giggling as he swung her arm back and forth making their way down the hallway, downstairs and through the kitchen.

Out in the open, Jack inhaled deeply the fresh salty air, exhilarated and peaceful. This beach seemed to instantly restore him each time he experienced the freedom of just "being" here. He vehemently hoped the change of scenery would have a similar effect on Gabriella's spirits. Not having kept track of Bree and Vinnie while up in his room, Jack turned in the opposite direction from where he had seen the pair walking earlier. Much as he wanted to reconnect with Bree and smooth things over with her, he needed to reserve this time for his little girl.

He plodded through the softer sand until reaching hard-packed footing at the ocean's edge while Gabriella kept abreast of him. The white noise of the undulating ocean filled his ears. Utterly content, Jack didn't feel the need to say a word. He sensed that Gabriella felt the same way judging from her loose limbed, seemingly happy gate and her bouncy, sporadic squatting to inspect seashells closer. Each time she found something worthy of slipping into her net bag, she sent him a victorious grin.

Only two females can melt my heart with a simple smile, he mused. He marveled at the good fortune that had blessed him in this land of Indian folklore and maritime treasures. Gabriella edged ahead of him and then spontaneously broke into a run. Her hair streaming behind her in a riot of raven curls, she pranced unfettered. He picked up his pace just enough to give her space and still keep her well in view as they approached a pier. Happiness surged through him watching his girl revel in the natural beauty that surrounded them.

Jack caught up with her when she plopped down on the sand just short of the pier, her slim legs stretched out in front of her, so that the water tickled her feet and ankles on the fringe of surf. Squatting down, he lowered onto his backside and sat beside her.

Neither spoke for several minutes, but Jack didn't obsess about her silence. Instead, he remained satisfied that he had broken his line of questioning about the accident just in time and had gotten her the hell out of that room to her healing place before undoing all the progress she had made this week.

Despite his relative confidence, when her voice came now, weak and timid, Jack registered shock almost equal to her first words a few evenings ago after the seemingly endless drought. "I did it, Daddy..."

Jack turned his head and squinted at her. "I'm sorry, sweetheart. What did you say?"

She stared at him, her eyes saucers. "I made Mommy stop looking at the cars."

Her chest heaved as she seemed to expend gargantuan effort to speak further, "I yelled at her." She sniffled, tears flowing anew. "She turned around... "And yelled at me," she choked out.

Gabriella hung her head. When she faced Jack, grief swam in her expressive eyes. The sorrow etched on her innocent face had his heart skipping a beat. "I don't understand. I *know* that it wasn't your fault. Please," he said, "I want you to stop thinking about it. OK?"

He patted her arm, grateful that she didn't shrink from his touch.

She frowned, wagging her head rapidly. "No Daddy. I want to tell you. She was saying mean things to you. I heard even with the earphones on. And I screamed Mommy *stop* fighting with Daddy. And...and she turned around and her eyes were so mean. She yelled, 'Just listen to your movie and...'"

"That's all right, sweetheart. You don't have to go on..."

"I'm not. That's all I heard." She tried to blink away tears to no avail. Sobbing now she managed, "Then I was in the hospital and you said Mommy went to heaven."

Jack closed his eyes as all the puzzle pieces assembled into a clear picture. That nasty voicemail message had ended Sophia's life and had put in motion Gabriella's unexpressed anguish. How alone his little girl must have felt all this time. He swept her into his lap and held her tightly against his chest. He murmured, "It wasn't your fault, darling. I love you so much. Mommy loves you so much. And she is looking down from heaven right this minute and I absolutely know what she wants to say to you."

Her upturned eyes held such tenuous hope that Jack was terrified he'd misstep in the next instant. *Where the hell is a shrink when I need one?* He half wished that Bree would stroll into view and come to his rescue—even if she were arm in arm with that thorn, Vinnie.

"You can hear Mommy talking to me? Like Skye can hear Charlie and Buddy the dolphins talking?"

OK, that's as good a save as any. "Sure. Kind of like that. Mommy is saying, 'Oh my baby girl, I can't believe you thought you made the accident happen! Not true! I'm so sorry that *I* made the accident happen. And so glad that you're all right and you're with Daddy. I *never* should have turned around to talk to you. Bad driving and against the rules. I hope you can forgive me for fighting with your Daddy.'"

"I can," she professed, wide-eyed.

"And I hope you can forgive me for fighting with Mommy," Jack added.

As if a switch flipped, she whipped her head sideways and pointed seaward with an outstretched arm. "Daddy *look*! Do you see the dolphins? Right there."

Jack followed along the line of her index finger and sighted several fins breaking the surface and then submerging. Gabriella bounded to her feet and Jack joined her in the vigil for a fresh sighting, hyper-focusing on the remembered spot beyond the breakers where he had last seen the creatures.

In seconds, they were rewarded with a surprising show when five dolphins surfed a cresting wave straight towards them. She squealed in delight as they disappeared underwater mere feet from where Jack and Gabriella stood on the shore.

"You didn't answer me, sweetheart. Can you forgive me for fighting with Mommy?"

"You bet," she replied with a sunny lilt in her voice.

Chapter 21

Bree poured Cabernet Sauvignon nearly up to the brim of the glass from the decanter on the sideboard, and then drifted over to the kitchen table. She pulled out two chairs, plopped down in one, extended her legs one at a time over the seat of the other chair and propped up her feet on the cushion. The tantalizing aromas of tangy tomato and pepper-minty basil scented the air. She swallowed a mouthful of wine.

What a roller coaster day. Only a few hours ago Jack entwined her hands in his and professed his love. Stunned at the depressing reversal, now she sipped a lonely glass of wine.

High heels clacked on the tile floor drawing Bree's attention. Kay, clad in a pastel, shoulder baring sundress, sashayed into the kitchen with Mike at her side. Clean-shaven and sporting chinos and a crisp cotton shirt, Mike beamed like the lucky man he was that a beauty like her mother had chosen him.

"Honey there's a spaghetti pie warming in the oven. Salad's in the fridge," Kay said, ever preoccupied with the stomachs of the Inn's occupants. "There's enough for you Skye, Jack and Ella, I think."

"There's enough for a battalion," Mike quipped, giving Bree a wink.

Kay leaned down and brushed a kiss on Bree's cheek. Her light floral perfume filled her senses: sweet, consoling—familiar. Unmistakably "mother" to Bree.

"You smell better than the dinner, Mom. Perfume and heels? What's the occasion?"

"It's date night," Mike said, wrapping an arm around Kay and drawing her close to his side, bumping hips.

Kay smiled up at him and then turned toward Bree. "I hope you don't mind taking over kitchen duty tonight, honey? You know I don't like to leave when we have guests, but this will probably be our last date night until after Labor Day."

"Of course I don't mind. Where are you guys going?"

"Some chick flick," Mike replied with a shake of his head. "But after, we're going to the grill for a nice big juicy cheeseburger." A that's-more-like-it grin lit his face.

"You kids have a great time. Don't stay out too late." Bree mimicked Mike's basso voice and his well used send off for one or the other of his daughter's dates.

Alone again with her wine, Bree watched a few stragglers out on the sand fold up their beach chairs and shake out their blankets. Her parents' example throughout her life confirmed that true love was real—attainable. She yearned to live a similar life of trust and unwavering love and date nights.

She gulped another mouthful of wine, dispirited to the core. How had she permitted Vinnie to disrupt something so important to her? Having found her deepest desires with Jack, now she might not live that yearned for life at all.

Skye breezed into the kitchen, yanked open the

refrigerator door and disappeared behind the gaping panel. Reemerging with an apple in hand, she leaned her left side against the counter, crunched a mouthful of fruit, lifted the glass dome covering a plate of brownies, and set the dome down on the counter. Sinking her teeth into the apple, she held it in her mouth while nabbing a brownie and then replacing the glass cover on the plate.

"You're going to spoil your appetite for dinner," Bree said, cringing at how much she sounded like their mother.

Skye's smile lit her face. "This *is* dinner. I have to run to the STAR center."

"Can't it wait until later this evening? I'd love the company."

"Uh-uh," she grunted, her mouth full of chocolate pastry. Skye chewed with an ecstatic expression on her face and then swallowed with an audible gulp. "Tomorrow we're releasing the girls back into the ocean. I want to go and spend some quiet time with them."

The pending turtle release publicity trended on Twitter and Facebook. STAR, Sea Turtle Assistance and Rehabilitation, at the aquarium had rapidly gained the national reputation of employing marine biologists who were veritable turtle whisperers. Specialists had successfully treated two loggerhead turtles after boat hits and the animals had recuperated enough for release "home". A crowd would assemble on the beach first thing in the morning for the bon voyage party. Her sensitive sister needed alone time to say her goodbyes.

"I saw Vinnie on his way out. I'm glad he's gone. The house feels calmer without his energy." Skye took another bite of brownie, the apple apparently usurped by a more excellent sugar high.

"You're too hard on him. He's a good guy, Skye. The shooting really wasn't his fault. I pressed him to let me go on that interview. We both miscalculated how unhinged the suspect would become. I'm actually more to blame than Vin. I profiled her, and I should have predicted her behavior."

Skye nodded. "I guess I know that. But he still gets under my skin. I don't see you with him, even though it's obvious that he wants that. He's not right for you." A sly smile lit her face as she stared out through the window, training her eyes in the distance. "Jack is the man I see in your life. A perfect match."

Bree followed Skye's gaze surprised to find that her sister didn't focus on the landscape, but rather the purported perfect man for her. In the foreground of her view, Jack led Ella to the outdoor spigot, turned the water on to gushing and took turns with his daughter rinsing sand off their feet.

"I don't think you're right about him, Skye." Bree set her glass down on the table, rose from her seat and drifted over to the kitchen counter across from Skye. "All we do is argue."

"Do you make up?"

"I guess we have so far. But I'm not so sure about the last disagreement."

"Trust me, you will."

"Skye, look what I found." Ella burst into the kitchen. She extended her arm. A tiny whelk nestled in her palm atop a small pile of sand granules. "It's perfect. Not one hole in it."

"What a great addition to your collection." Skye

rounded the counter and knelt on the floor inspecting the offered whelk as if it were a valuable heirloom.

Having been indoctrinated by Kay since toddlerhood to the intricacies involved in shell formulation—the amazing symmetry, coloration and mind-boggling variety—the Layton sisters believed seashells *were* priceless heirlooms.

"Wanna come with me to wash it and add it to my other shells?"

"I wish I could, but I have to go to the aquarium. I want to say good bye to a couple of friends tonight."

"What friends?"

Skye stood up, handed the seashell back to Ella and brushed her hands along the length of her thighs sending a sprinkle of sand down to the floor. "Remember, I told you about the rescued turtles yesterday?"

Ella's eyes widened, alight with recognition. "Oh, yes. Mavis and Minerva."

Turning towards Jack, Ella explained, "A boat ran them over. Before the STAR center, people who watched out for turtles and their nests, like Miss Kay, took care of injured turtles in their houses!"

Sounding like a mini school teacher she continued her lecture, "Now they have a real hospital and special tanks and everything. The doctors at the turtle hospital helped Mavis and Minerva. Tomorrow they will send them back to their homes in the ocean and have a party on the beach. Daddy, can we please go to the party?"

"I think that can be arranged, sweetheart."

"Yay!" Ella threw her arms around Jack, closed her eyes and squeezed.

Jack stroked her glossy hair and she smiled up at

him adoringly. His broad smile and sparkling eyes conveyed mutual adoration to his little girl.

Bree's chest constricted. She yearned for Jack to train adoring eyes on her again.

He touched Ella gently on the shoulder. "How about you go take care of that new shell upstairs and wash your hands for dinner? It smells like we're in for another special meal."

"I'll see you both in the morning, Ella. We can go to the release together, if you like, Jack," Skye said as she stooped to give Ella a hug.

"Sure," he said.

Skye grabbed a bottle of water out of the fridge and trailed Ella out of the kitchen.

Jack stood only a few feet away, but Bree felt separated from him by miles. Her hands hung limply at her sides. She itched to say or do something that would bridge this gap and rewind to their lovely togetherness earlier in the day.

He remained immobile, facing the archway and seemed intent on ignoring her. Suddenly, he spun on his heel, strode over to Bree and swept her into a twirling embrace. "I think she's beyond hearing range now," he said.

Her thoughts scrambled and her spirit soared at the spontaneous new reversal. He released her after several spins to a soft landing. His arms still draped around her offering warmth, comfort and that indefinable, heady rush that only Jack could engender. Dizzy literally and figuratively she said, "What was that all about?"

"You're not going to believe what happened and I have you and Skye and this extraordinary place to thank for it. Ella finally opened up. She told me what happened the day Sophia died."

Thrilled, Bree said, "That's a critical breakthrough."

Perfectly happy to assume that all things Vinnie were forgiven by this marvelous development, Bree grinned up at him. "Want to join me with a glass of wine?"

At his nod, she paced to the sideboard, filled a goblet with wine and handed it to Jack. Bree returned to her place at the table, sat down and patted the seat next to her. "Sit. Tell me everything."

He took a swig of the wine, grabbed the back wrung of the chair with one hand, twirled it around and straddled it. Jack in motion screamed virility to Bree. Again, just his physical nearness set steamy fantasies ablaze in her mind.

His eyes soft, she could almost feel the excitement emanating from him. "Ella was playing with her shell collection and she talked about how much she loves Skye... and you. Even though you're not magic, and I guess she thinks Skye is." He rolled his eyes at what he apparently viewed as absurdity.

Bree forced herself not to react. She should set him straight and corroborate Ella's belief. Soon.

"Although I was afraid she'd shut me out again, I felt strongly that the time was right to broach the subject. I asked her if she would talk to me about the day her mother died." He sandwiched her hand between his. "And she did."

Bree relished the physical and emotional connection to Jack as he related the details of the breakthrough. She didn't want this intimacy to end. But his vacation here rapidly drew to a close. The uncertainty of where they went from here hung over her head like a guillotine blade. Should she offer her neck with revealing the reality behind Sisters of the Legend?

"When she finally told me her version of the facts of the accident she said, 'I did it.' She felt responsible for making her mother turn around while driving."

"Oh no. I suspected as much. What did you say to convince her otherwise?"

"I told her I could hear her mother talking from Heaven."

"Hmm…" Suggesting the possibility of discourse with a deceased loved one might backfire. Ella could become dispirited when her mommy didn't talk specifically to her.

"I know that sounds strange, especially from me," Jack continued, "But she immediately equated it to Skye's tales of talking to animals. Thank God that Skye included Gabriella in her make-believe world. I kind of winged it like Skye and put words in Sophia's mouth. She told Gabriella that she wasn't to blame for the accident at all—it was the other way around. Sophia was responsible with her bad driving."

Jack leaned towards her, his rounded eyes fairly begging her for a positive response to his narrative.

Bree stared at the wine in her glass.

"What? Did I do something wrong? Should I not have made that stuff up?"

"It's not that. What you did for Ella is healing. She needed to know that her mother didn't blame her for the accident. And you couldn't let her continue to believe that she was responsible. All in all, I think the way you conveyed that was effective." Bree continued to contemplate her wine glass rather than meet his eyes.

"I hear a big but coming…"

"Honestly, I think you handled Ella's confidence exactly right," she said lightly. *But you're dead wrong about Skye's so called make-believe world.*

Now or never. A wave of nausea swelled inside Bree at the thought. Regardless, she believed that if this relationship had any chance to grow Jack needed to know the whole truth about her family, her history and her role in the ancient Legend. He had given her the perfect opening to start the conversation. She took a deep breath.

Chapter 22

"Yes, there's a 'but'. Did you read one of the pamphlets we have in the parlor about the Legend of the Three Butterflies?'

Jack nodded. "Yeah, your dad gave me one. It's a great promo piece for this place. Binding spells and all that. Like haunted house ads for Halloween."

"It's not promo. It's my family history," she said softly.

Bree closed her eyes and held her breath. She didn't want to see the shock on his face as the implications registered...and multiplied in his imagination.

"What are you trying to tell me? The triplets...turned into butterflies. You and your sisters..." The volume of his voice rose successively after each breath he took between utterances. "It's a fable, *right*?" he thundered.

"Don't yell at me," she thundered back. And then she stared directly at him. "It's not a fable. It's literally the account of how my ancestors, um, settled on OBX."

He gaped at her. "What the hell...?"

"In each generation of the Binder family since then, female triplets were born with... special powers."

"Binder family? Your name..."

"Mom's name is Kay Binder Layton," she interjected. "Mine is Breeze Binder Layton, and so forth."

"Oh come on, Bree. This is ridiculous. Why are you bullshitting me?"

Quaking inside, Bree held her tongue. When her parents fell in love, Dad had received this same revelation about Mom with…yes, incredulity at first, but then a sense of wonder…almost reverence. When your normal is paranormal from birth on, you accept it—take it for granted, even though you understand that you're not *exactly* normal by everyone else's standards. Like having a psychic parent…or a clairvoyant. She had always considered her heritage special. And it absolutely was *not* bullshit.

Bree slapped her hand on the table with a resonant crack. And then she surged to her feet. The momentum thrust her chair into the wall creating a racket as if someone ransacked the place. She glared at him. "This. Conversation. Is. Over."

Balling her hands into fists she propped them on the table and leaned forward. Her gaze boring into his storm cloud eyes, she said, "I thought you felt the same way about me as I…," she sputtered, close to tears. "I wanted you to know everything about me. No secrets. No surprises."

She shoved away from the table and headed toward the back stairs.

"Bree, stop!"

No, you stop, she thought. She picked up her pace and reached the bottom riser in three strides.

As she was about to climb the stairs, he grasped her arm from behind pulling her up short. She spun to face him.

"Let go of me, Jack," she snapped, her voice an

echoing boom. She twisted her arm to escape his clutch.

"Please, wait," he whispered.

The tenderness in his eyes gave her pause. She held still while prepared to wrest free from him at the least provocation.

"I'm sorry."

That at least, was a proper start.

"Can you please explain further? I promise to keep my mind open and my mouth shut."

Bree smiled at that as she debated complying. What if he didn't love her enough to hold secret the truth of her ancestry? Could he hurt her family? Beyond breaking her heart...

"Trust me," he pleaded.

The honesty that she read in his eyes tugged at Bree's heart. If she wanted a future with Jack she had no choice but to reveal all. The idea of a future without Jack appalled her. No choice.

"I've never told anyone the whole story before."

"Not even old pal, Vinnie?" The bite of sarcasm contradicted his smile.

Still, a smile had never been so irresistible. Her heart had never been so totally *owned* by a man. "No one. Because I've never loved anyone the way I love you."

He enfolded her in his arms. She allowed the peace and rightness of this shelter to overtake any lingering misgivings. He was the only one she could ever trust with her secrets and her heart.

"So...you mentioned special powers," he said.

She arched her neck and looked up at him. "Right."

"Right now I have nothing but questions." He grinned. "Want to go sit back down and explain this to me?"

"Sure."

Seated across from him at the table she said, "We're direct descendants of John and Sarah mentioned in the brochure on my mother's side of the family. My mom has two sisters."

Jack arched his eyebrows. "Identical sisters?

"Yep, my mom is an identical triplet."

"Wow. OK. What about this whole butterfly thing?"

"Out of the triplets in each generation, one has the most power. The other two might have a more enlightened intuition or the ability to predict. Of the three of us, Skye has the most power. She isn't pretending to talk to animals. She really can talk to animals."

Bree's heart skipped a beat and she hesitated to expound further. All her adult life she had dreaded this moment. "She can turn into an animal herself." *And she can turn me and Summer into animals, too.*

"Can your mom talk to animals, too?"

Either he hadn't heard her or it hadn't penetrated enough for him to throw the bullshit card again. "No, but her sister Karol can. Her other sister Kamille has the same powers as my mom, Summer, and me."

"OK."

Was it, Bree thought? Jack blinked his eyes several times as he wagged his head.

"Are you all right? Still want to see me when we're back in Chicago?"

"I don't intend to let you go, Bree." He leaned forward and kissed her cheek. "But, this is a lot to digest. I've never dated a witch before."

"Wait. I'm not a witch. We're perfectly normal people with a little...extra."

"You mean Mrs. Kravitz won't peek into our windows and you don't wiggle your nose to turn people into frogs or whatever?"

Bree hooted a laugh, warmed by the idea that they'd share windows in the future. "No, Jack. Our life together won't be anything like an episode of *Bewitched*."

"It already is. You bewitch me." He rose from his chair and drew her up into an embrace. Her heart leaped at the expression in his eyes.

"Every time we're together, I fall deeper in love with you, Bree."

"I love you more and more, too, Jack. Let's not fight anymore, OK?"

"Deal."

His lips met hers, a slow, gentle, blood-stirring kiss. Hungry for more, she deepened the kiss lacing her arms around his neck. Her heart hammered in her chest and her mind swirled. He had accepted her truth. Nothing stood in the way of having everything she had ever dreamed come true with Jack.

He separated from her slowly. "Let's get dinner on the table fast," he said. "The sooner Gabriella is in bed; the sooner we can continue this where we left off."

His husky voice sent shivers through her.

"Great idea," she agreed.

Bree handed Jack two potholders. He opened the oven door, lifted the bubbling casserole out and placed it on the hot plate on the table while Bree grabbed three plates out of the cupboard. The cell phone in her back pocket vibrated and buzzed.

She slid out the phone and checked the screen. "It's Summer." The message read, *is everything all right?*

Bree smiled. Her sister must have sensed the roller coaster emotions that had pulsed through Bree the past hour.

All good, Bree typed. She hit send.

Before she returned the phone back into her pocket, it buzzed again.

Assuming Summer had something further to say, she was surprised to see "Mom" display as the sender. Especially with the identical text she had just received from Summer, *Is everything all right?*

Goosebumps raised on Bree's arm and a shiver ran up her spine. Was the off-center feeling that engulfed her residual dizziness from Jack's kiss? This seemed different.

A third message signal buzzed. Skye's text read, WHERE IS ELLA?

****

Bree snapped her focus away from the phone screen to Jack's eyes. Her furrowed brow and the clouds in her jade eyes had his pulse accelerating instinctively. "Is something wrong?" he asked intuiting that she'd answer, yes.

"I don't know." She sprang up from the chair, bounded to the built-in desk on the other side of the room and picked up a portable phone.

She punched in four numbers and then gazed ahead, a vacant expression in her eyes, listening. After a couple seconds, she took the phone away from her ear and redialed.

"She's not in her room," she advised Jack. "At least she didn't answer the phone."

His concern growing, Jack rose from his seat. 'She' had to refer to his daughter. "Who, Gabriella? What were those texts about?"

Bree nodded, the phone pressed to her ear. "Jack, she's not answering the phone in your room, either." She hung up, clattering the portable onto the desktop.

"Maybe she's on her way downstairs." He frowned. Why was Bree so alarmed by the texts?

"I'll take the back stairs; you go up front?" Bree said already in motion.

Still confused, Jack sped to the designated staircase and bounded up to the second floor, two steps at a time. Bree sprinted down the long hallway from the opposite direction. She reached his rooms a split second before him and pounded three times on Gabriella's door. "Honey, it's Bree," she called out.

Jack edged next to Bree and inserted his key in the lock and preceded her through the door. In two seconds he determined that Gabriella wasn't there. He spun around facing Bree. "What's happening? You received texts about Gabriella?"

Her hands on her hips and her chest heaving, Bree nodded. "Mom and Summer texted, is everything all right? Then Skye's text read, where's Ella in caps. They obviously saw something. Where could she have gone, Jack?"

"What do you mean 'saw something'? I'm..." The import that his daughter had inexplicably gone missing in the last fifteen minutes slammed the breath out of him.

In the next second, he raced out of the room on a bead for an exit. Thudding feet sounded from behind as Bree joined his pursuit. Descending the front stairs in leaps, he sped through the parlor and shoved the front door open. Since he and Bree had occupied the kitchen when the texts came in, Gabriella had to have used the front exit for whatever reason. Halting at the curb he scanned both directions down the two-lane road in the dim light.

He faced Bree. "Do you think she went around to the beach?"

"We can check."

Headlights swept the apron as the Inn's van pulled up and jerked to a halt in the driveway. The passenger door burst open and Kay emerged. She hopped down onto the driveway and hastened towards them.

"Did you see, Mom?"

"Yes," she said, her voice strained, breathless. "Randy Wyatt took her."

"*What?*" Jack bellowed. "Kay, he kidnapped my little girl? How could this be?"

Kay clasped Bree's hands. "They're at the Wyatt marina."

Jack recoiled at the news. He *had* to act, but in that instant his brain seemingly froze. Rooted to the spot, he didn't even flinch when headlights shone directly in his eyes. A jeep screeched to a halt with a spray of gravel at the front curb.

"Get in," Skye commanded.

Grateful that a course of action had magically presented, Jack slipped into the passenger seat while Bree jumped into the back.

"You know where to go?" Bree asked.

Skye nodded while she stared straight ahead through the windshield, eagle-eyed. "He has her on the boat. She's fine. Scared. But unhurt."

214

This is insane. *Insane, insane.*

Bree said, "Vinnie..."

"He's there," Skye interjected. "On a wide perimeter. There are at least ten agents with him."

Bumping around in the front seat in the speeding car, Jack followed the interchange without fully comprehending. His mind inflated with ballooning panic as they approached the boatyard and Skye suddenly cut the lights. She pulled over a hundred yards short of the Wyatts' parking area.

At last free to act, Jack leapt out of the jeep and stalked towards the marina, unaware of anyone or anything other than finding his little girl. A shadow moved in front of him, loomed, and materialized into human form. A large hand grabbed his arm roughly and yanked him sideways. Thrown off balance, Jack was shoved behind a parked car before he could resist. The man forced Jack into a crouch and then crouched next to him.

"Stay here until I tell you otherwise," the man whispered.

Identifying Vinnie's voice, Jack reared back to deliver a punch. Vinnie deflected the blow, capturing Jack's fist in his hand. "Listen," he whispered urgently, "this operation is happening, and I won't let you interfere. What are you doing here?"

"I don't know how or why, but my daughter is on one of those boats..."

Gravel crunched with pounding footfalls behind him. Jack turned and spied Bree and Skye running across the road, hands linked. In the next instant, two white pelicans took flight and soared overhead. Wings spanning at least seven feet per bird seemed joined at the tips as if holding hands.

Jack sat back on his haunches in the road as the insanity increased twofold.

Chapter 23

Bree had no idea why Ella had left nor what had driven Randy to take her. Because of the earlier sighting from the charter boat, Bree's conscience pricked her with guilt. Soaring over the pier with Skye, Bree only knew that she had to do everything in her power to set things right.

Skye had figured Ella weighed probably less than sixty and surely no more than seventy pounds. Together they could do this. In this body, even from these heights, Bree could spot fish below the surface of the water that lapped the pier. Amazing how clear the panorama below her appeared. Almost immediately, she spied Ella, a dark, small bundle, huddled in the bow of *Gofish 1*. Two hunched figures transferred crates from the pier to the aft deck in the gloom. Standing upright on the deck, a man, who had to be Randy, gestured as if directing the other two.

"Got her, do you?" Bree clearly received Skye's mental telepathy.

"Yes," Bree said. "How will we do this?"

"Leave that to me. Stay with me, okay?"

Skye nose-dived toward the boat and Bree followed in her wake. If the purpose of this transformation weren't dead serious Bree would have reveled in the freefall and the first time experience of pelican flight. The power and sheer agility of slicing through the salty air proved heady. Flitting and dipping in butterfly form suffered in comparison.

"Going to slow down here," came Skye's mental transference as she ended the plummet.

Bree followed suit and then tailed Skye over the boat, aft to fore. Swooping towards Ella, Skye dipped lower, a whoosh of air over the little girl's crown. Ella raised her head skyward as Bree passed over her. Skye circled back for another pass and then another, while Bree flew lazy circles above the boat channel.

Skye approached Bree's position. "I got through to her. You fly the line on her right side. I go in on the left. Stay parallel with me the whole way. When we have her, head towards the shallows. I don't want to risk dropping her over land. Go."

Ella now stood facing them, arms extended at ninety-degree angles to her sides. As Bree neared the vessel, Ella's radiant smile gave her courage. But all the wing flapping at the rear had apparently drawn Randy's attention. Brandishing a spear, he lumbered toward the stern.

Adrenaline coursed through her. In a split second, she decided to attack him and trust Ella to Skye. No words needed with her sister, Bree accelerated flying the direct line to her target. Randy raised the spear as she barreled forward on a collision course with his bulky torso. His arm angled backward ready to set the javelin in flight.

Blinding floodlights suddenly illuminated him, the boat, the contraband, and the surrounding fishing fleet in the marina. An amplified voice boomed, "FBI. Don't move."

Randy froze in place, providing a brick wall to

Bree's trajectory. She slammed into him beak first. The spear flew out of his hands and clattered against the cabin wall before landing innocuously on deck.

Randy caved inward, fell to his knees with cap shattering dual thunks and then sprawled on his face. Stunned, Bree ricocheted off his body and flopped onto the deck. She lay on the smooth deck floor, gathering her wits and preparing to reverse the spell. A cacophony of heavy boots pounded the wooden boards of the pier. Two splashes sounded. Skye had succeeded in rescuing Ella.

Beyond grateful and satisfied that she had dealt Randy a solid blow, Bree mustered her energy for another first—transmogrification without Skye's help. She figured if Skye had imbued her with the power to transform, she possessed the power to revert.

Bree managed to return to self, a cyclonic host of sensations just short of torture. Her breathing was shallow and despite her strong intentions to get up, run to the railing and determine if Skye needed further help, she couldn't move out of her position curled on her side.

Heavy footfalls sounded, vibrating the floorboards under her ear. "Breeze!"

The vibrations increased and the thudding pounded closer and closer. Vinnie's face swam into view, arching over her. He stooped down and clasped her shoulders, lifting her head gently off the deck.

"What the hell happened here?" He tipped his head in Randy's direction.

Bree clutched Vinnie's triceps and sat up. Rising, he slid his hands down her arms to grasp both her hands and towed her to her feet. Wobbly, she leaned on him.

"Go slow," he said.

Her head cleared within seconds. Making good on earlier intentions, she sped to the railing. The glare on deck impeded the view of the Sound and the shoreline beyond the pool of spillover light on the water's surface near the boat. Despite lacking positive confirmation, Bree had no doubt that Skye had brought Ella to safety.

Vinnie grunted. Bree turned to see him shove his arm under Randy's shoulders and heave him up to his feet. He gave him a push forward toward a pair of Agents clad in the same dark clothes as Vinnie. "Here you go. Cuff him. He's Wyatt's son."

He narrowed his eyes and regarded Bree. "Are you responsible for Wyatt landing on his ass or what?"

Bree snorted. "Something like that."

She strolled over to him and linked her arm through his. "It's a long story. Maybe some time I'll tell it to you."

"You've got to be shitting me. How did you breach my perimeter and board this boat without my seeing you? By yourself? Why? You really took Wyatt on by yourself? What on God's green earth *possessed* you? You knew the operation was going down tonight. Why would you even get *involved*? This has nothing to do with you..."

Bree realized that she had crossed a line. Vinnie's questioning would inevitably lead to accusing her of police interference. "I'm sorry. I'm not taking this lightly. Truth is, I acted without thinking. Randy kidnapped Gabriella and I was panic-stricken. I didn't even think about your operation."

"Geez. What is this perp into besides drug running? Branching out into human trafficking? Wait..." The furrow in his brow was a canyon. "Let me get this straight..."

He paused. Seconds ticked off and his silence was more intimidating than his interrogation.

"OK...was Skye involved in this little—caper?"

Bree weighed the advisability of denial. But he had to know something or he wouldn't have posed the question. "Yes," she conceded. "Why?"

"Because she strolled up to lover boy holding the little girl's hand. His reaction was to grab hold of the kid like he'd never let go. This was after he had sat on the ground for about fifteen minutes looking like he had been hit over the head with a sledgehammer. I pulled him over and made him crouch down, but I didn't put that look on his face."

"Well then, you have your answers."

"Bullshit. The two of you went vigilante? And, by the way, I neglected to say that the kid's hair and clothes were soaking wet. Skye didn't have a drop on her. Want to explain that?"

"What did Skye say to Jack?"

"I didn't hang around to hear. I had a job to do. What do *you* think Skye said to Jack?"

"Hmm..." Bree said. "Probably that Skye turned us both into pelicans and we stormed the boat. I hammered Randy with my beak while Skye helped Ella to jump overboard. And then Skye turned into a dolphin and towed Ella to shore. And then turned back into Skye. And I helped you get your man. So how could you be mad at me?"

Vinnie guffawed as he tugged her lightly forward. "Now you're *really* bullshitting me. Come on. Skye drove off with your boyfriend. Wanted to get Ella in a hot shower. I'll take you home. But first we're stopping at Outer Banks Hospital. Your nose is swollen. Might be broken. Pretty sure you're working on two beauts of shiners, too."

Bree touched her nose gently. Pain pounded straight into her skull. She closed her eyes a few seconds until the throbbing diminished to a dull ache. "All right," she agreed.

"And I want to take your statement about the child abduction. This guy's going away for a long time."

Chapter 24

Jack's hands would not stop shaking. He sat on the edge of the tub while Gabriella, apparently bubbling with excitement, regaled him with her take on pelicans to the rescue.

"Daddy, it was so amazing. I heard wings flapping and I looked up and saw two pelicans flying towards me. Then I heard Skye's voice in my head—really clear. She told me not to be afraid. The pelicans were going to save me. And I wasn't afraid or anything."

Grateful that at least one of them had emerged from the ordeal emotionally unscathed, Jack used the plush washcloth to squeeze warm water down her back.

"Then I heard Skye tell me to close my eyes, and I did, and then all of a sudden, I was in the water sitting on a dolphin. Can you believe it, Daddy? I road on a dolphin's back." Her saucer eyes and huge grin radiated pure awe.

Jack's take, however, was more like pure horror.

"It *is* hard to believe," he said evenly, hoping he didn't project the repulsion swirling inside him.

His heart continued to race as it had from the moment two pelicans took flight right next to him where two women had stood before. Although overwhelmingly grateful that Skye and Bree had brought his daughter to safety, their shape-shifting left him aghast—and determined to shield Gabriella from this strange and inexplicable reality. How had *any* of this happened?

"Why did you leave the Inn? I was so worried when I couldn't find you. I thought you were up in your room."

Her shoulders sagged and tears welled. She bowed her head and sniffled.

Jack's heart skipped a beat witnessing her dismay. "Please don't cry, sweetheart. I'm not angry with you. I just want to understand. Did something happen that made you want to leave me?"

"The fighting." She hunched over, so small. So vulnerable.

"What fighting?"

"I came downstairs for dinner and…" She lifted her head and gazed into his eyes. "I heard you and Bree yelling at each other. Just like you and Mommy used to do."

Gabriella covered her eyes and sobbed. Bubbles glistened on the backs of her fingers reflecting overhead light.

"Oh my poor baby." In a rush, he stood and reached into the tub, wrapping his arms around her trembling body. Scooping her out of the water, he lowered to a sitting position on the bathroom floor, cradling her in his lap. He draped a soft, oversized towel around her shoulders and held her tight.

"I'm sorry you overheard Bree and me arguing, but people do disagree sometimes. Then they say they're sorry and make up."

"Did you and Bree make up?" The hope shining in the wide eyes she trained on him pierced his heart.

"We did. I apologized for raising my voice." He

wiped tears off her cheeks with the edge of the towel. "Feel better?"

She nodded and then knit her brow. "I'm sorry I ran away. I thought I could find Skye. Then that mean man drove next to me. And he said he would drive me to the aquarium. I shouldn't have believed him."

Her lips quivered and her voice broke.

He hastened to reassure her. "Shh... It's over now. But you can never run off like that again, sweetheart. Promise me that if something is wrong or something bothers you; you will run *to* me."

"I promise. I was so scared until Skye came." She yawned as she snuggled closer to his chest.

"Let's get you to bed. We have to get up in a few hours to catch our flight."

"We're leaving?"

"We are. I got a call from work," he improvised. "We have to leave sooner than we planned."

"But what about the turtles? Skye said we could go with her for the home-going party."

"I'll ask Skye to video the release for us. That way you can kind of go to the party as many times as you want."

Her silence hopefully meant that he had appeased her. Setting her on her feet, he left the bathroom while she put on her pajamas. Jack stayed with Gabriella until she fell asleep. Slipping back into his room he packed his suitcase. Then he crept back into her room and gathered her things.

After treading through the hallway and down the stairs in his stocking feet, he eased open the front door. He made a quick round trip to his car to stow the luggage and then sat in the parlor hanging over his cell phone. A couple of clicks in the airline app later, he had secured two first class tickets on the earliest morning flight out of Norfolk to Chicago. The sooner he put distance between himself and Bree the better.

Pain ballooned inside at the necessity to abandon Bree. True, Jack loved this special woman. But nothing prepared him for just how...special...

Jack cupped his forehead and applied pressure to his aching temples. No matter the inner turmoil, he had to leave. He checked his watch and determined that he had enough time to jump in the shower before the two-hour drive to the airport.

****

Head-splitting pain wracked Bree at awakening. She cautiously lifted her head off her pillow and instantly regretted it. Clapping her hand over her mouth she muffled a groan. Flipping the covers off, she swung her legs over the side of the mattress. Splayed halfway out of bed, she more or less slid to her feet and stood upright swaying in place.

Skye slept peacefully across their room. Regaining her equilibrium, Bree tiptoed forward and plucked shorts and a t-shirt out of the basket of clean clothes in the corner. She had collapsed last night fully dressed after coming home from the hospital. Although her head still swam, not one second of last night's events escaped her.

Raw, bruised and dreading facing that day, Bree brushed her teeth, splashed water on her face, and swallowed two aspirins before leaving her room.

Even though the light was on in the kitchen, the room was empty. A white envelope with her name scrawled on it was propped on the counter against a bowl of fresh fruit. She already knew what the envelope held—that's where the dread came in. She had heard movement downstairs sometime in her sleepless night. Then the sound of an engine turning had confirmed her suspicions. Jack had left her.

She slit the envelope open with a knife and extracted the single sheet of the Inn's stationery.

Dear Bree, I'm sorry to leave like this, but I have to remove Gabriella from tonight's trauma as quickly as possible. She seems okay, but I can't let anything set her back. I want her to finally have a normal life. I hope you can understand that.

I said that I would have an open mind about you, and your sisters' gifts, but tonight—I don't know what to say, except that this is not the life I want for my daughter.

I will always be grateful to you and your family for bringing my little girl back to me.

It hurts like hell to leave you; I hope you know that. And I hope you can forgive me.

Love, Jack

****

Bree calmly folded the paper and stuffed his letter back into the envelope. And then she crushed the envelope in her fist and tossed it towards the wastebasket, sinking the wad of paper with a swish. Biting back tears she donned a baseball cap, charged out the door and flew down the deck stairs, sinking barefoot into the cool sand.

Alone on the beach, tears flowed unchecked as she jogged, the physical exertion somehow necessary after reading Jack's goodbye. Crimson streaks painted the horizon. The muscles in her legs stretched and the beauty of the morning helped to ease the pain in her skull. Not so much her heart, but... Would she have done anything differently in helping Skye rescue Ella, given the chance?

No. She had drawn on the power of the Sacred Source as was meant—to protect. She didn't regret anything—except giving her heart to the wrong man. Instead of fleeing, Jack should want at least to thank Skye this morning.

Good thing she had learned this costly lesson about Jack. She was way better off without him.

Yeah, keep telling yourself that, and eventually, you might believe it.

Her family was more important than any man and with their help she would move on. She had to trust that there was someone out there like her dad. Someone who would love all of her—and even marvel at her wondrous abilities. Had she believed that man was Jack? Wholeheartedly.

Wrong.

She halted and spun a 180 for the reverse jog home. Bree allowed herself one last sob and then she swiped beneath her eyes with the back of her hand resolving not to cry over a six-day beach fling. If Jack could view things that way, she could, too.

Gazing at the spectacularly illuminated horizon, she whispered a prayer of gratitude for her special family and for the power that enabled Ella's rescue before she sprinted back to the Inn.

Skye sat on the lowest step leading up to the deck squinting up at her. "Morning. How are you feeling?"

"Actually, better." Bree tentatively touched her hand to her nose and winced. "Well, maybe not."

She observed Skye closely. "Look at you, not a mark on your face."

"I know better than to lead with my beak." Skye arched her eyebrows.

Bree burst out laughing at the absurdity of that sentence. She plopped down to sit next to Skye.

"How funny was Randy's face when we came swooping in? The Agents thought he was under the influence when he tried to explain what happened on the boat," Bree said.

Skye hooted a laugh. "I'm excited that you unbound by yourself and didn't need my help."

"I didn't think I could do it. Wait until Summer hears. She'll be so jealous."

"What am I going to be jealous about?" came the familiar voice.

Squealing Bree and Skye jumped up and rushed up the stairs to hug their sister.

"What are you doing here?"

"How did you get here?"

"After I texted you, Bree, I couldn't shake the feeling that you were in serious trouble. I was in a state of panic, and I called Mom. We went back and forth a couple times with updates, which finally led me to Vinnie. I almost lost it when I found out you were at the hospital.

"The man is impressive. He didn't hesitate to act. He got me on the FBI plane out of LaGuardia with his boss's boss, I think. I landed in Manteo a few hours ago. I missed…

"Whoa…" Summer stared steadfastly at Bree. "My god, your face. Are you all right?"

Bree gave her a sheepish grin. "Yeah, I'll live."

"Tell me everything."

Summer listened intently to Skye's narrative. While Skye spoke, Bree relived the evening in her thoughts, focusing on the success of their mission—not the failure of her romance.

"You're right, Bree. I'm totally jealous that you can unbind. Maybe I can learn." She narrowed her eyes. "Boy, your nose looks sore."

"It looks worse than it is."

"How are Ella and Jack? Is she very shaken up? He must be overwhelmed with relief."

"They're gone." Bree's breath caught in her throat at the admission.

"What?!" Summer and Skye cried out.

"Jack left a note. Basically, he said we're too weird to be around his daughter."

"No way!" Summer said.

"I might be paraphrasing, but the intent was clear. He bundled up Ella and slunk out in the middle of the night. I heard them go."

"Well, damn. I really thought you two were perfect together." Summer shook her head.

Skye remained uncharacteristically silent.

"I know what will make you feel better. When I came through the kitchen, Mom had the waffle iron heating up," Summer said. "I'm thinking…"

"Chocolate chip waffles with vanilla ice cream," the triplets chorused.

During their childhood, Kay instinctively knew when the girls needed a boost of chocolate to make them feel better at the beginning of a new day. Chocolate chip waffles with ice cream was the remedy. And today was definitely that day for Bree.

****

After over-indulging at breakfast, the triplets barreled into the backseat of Mike's car, shoulder to shoulder. Skye took her place in the middle, reminiscent of family road trips. The official peace keeper for the trio as youngsters, Kay always seated her between Bree and Summer who otherwise would poke each other and battle non-stop.

Bree pushed the button to open her window, hoping that the briny breeze fanning her face would clear her head. Regardless, thoughts of Jack and Ella, what they were missing today, and what she was missing today nagged her.

Mike pulled into the parking lot across from the lighthouse at Coquina beach. The Ranger had parked his dusty white truck near a sand dune. The sea turtles, Mavis and Minerva, occupied two black plastic tubs stowed in the bed of the pickup truck.

Bree and Summer said hello to the Park Ranger and then climbed over the dune to find a good position among the crowd milling on the beach. Both Skye and Kay served as devoted Network for Endangered Sea Turtles or NEST volunteers orchestrating the release. Mike was designated the photographer in charge of uploading videos and images to the NEST website. The Park Ranger's truck crested the dune and stopped thirty feet from the water's edge. The crowd parted to let the volunteers from the aquarium place the tubs on the sand.

Two STAR Center volunteers first hoisted Minerva out of the tub. The turtle worked her flippers rapidly while Kay followed her, toting a sign summarizing her vital information: weight, date rescued and injuries given attention. In minutes, the waves swallowed the creature.

Given her turn, Mavis apparently was in no hurry to reach the surf. Situated on the sand, she kept turning her head towards Skye who, like Kay, positioned at the rear with an information sign in hand. Skye's lips were moving. Bree knew that her sister voiced encouragement to the turtle to leave her and return home.

Bree and her sisters had participated in scores of these releases having served as STAR Center volunteers in their teens. Caring for these beautiful creatures made their releases bittersweet, albeit magical.

Mavis looked one last time at Skye and then plunged under the waves. Applause erupted from the onlookers. Moved to tears, Bree hugged Summer whose eyes also glistened with welling tears. Then they laughed together spontaneously, expressing their predictable conflicting emotions during turtle releases. Mike focused his camera on them and they struck a pose waving at him.

Trudging through the sand back to the car, Summer draped her arm over Bree's shoulder. "Since Jack is gone, are you leaving for Chicago now, too?"

How heartbreaking to think that going home could have meant being with Jack forever.

"No...." Maybe a few more days licking her wounds would help. "I'll fly home as planned. How about you? Can you stay with me?"

"Now that I know you're okay, I'm hitching a ride on a late night flight with Vinnie."

Bree's eyes brimmed tears.

Alarm swam in Summer's jade eyes. "Don't cry, sweetie. I'll stay if you need me."

Bree wagged her head. "No, no. I'm over-emotional. I'll miss you. And I'm so thankful that you came."

"I would have been here even if I had to drive all night. And we still have the whole day to play. Mom said she'll make a big dinner for all of us tonight, so no need for goodbyes just yet."

"I love you, Summer."

"Right back at you, sis."

Chapter 25

"Jackson, what are you doing here?" Jeannie Murphy gaped up at Jack from her desk chair.

He beamed his secretary a smile. "Last time I checked this place has my name on it. Has the Board ousted me since I've been gone?"

"Oh my gosh, no. It's just that I didn't expect you until Wednesday at the earliest."

I didn't expect that, either. "I guess Gabriella and I had enough sand and sea," he said lightly, positive that he'd never relate the real reason for cutting his vacation short to any other living soul.

She shoved back her chair, the castors scraping along the plastic carpet guard beneath her desk, and popped up. "Let me get you an espresso."

"Beat you to it," he said holding out a Starbucks cup. "I think I'll start the day sorting through my email. Anything else pressing?"

Jeannie wagged her head. "Nope. Zilch on the calendar and crisis in check."

"Good, thanks."

He breezed past her desk into his office. Jeannie followed on his heels. "What did you think of the Outer Banks? Are you glad I suggested a trip there? Wasn't it pure magic?"

The last, an extremely loaded question for Jack. "I am glad for the suggestion, and...Yes, it was magical."

The memory of soaring birds overhead the night of Gabriella's kidnapping and the fishbowl nature of the floor to ceiling glass walls of his office, high above the Chicago cityscape, combined into a sudden rush of dizziness. Shaken, Jack tucked into his leather-rolling chair, scooted forward and propped his elbows on his ebony desk for support.

She didn't pick up on his distress. "I knew you'd love it." She grinned. "Was it good for Gabriella? I lit a candle for her and for you at church last Sunday."

Jeannie's sweet intentions warmed his aching heart. "Thank you. Your prayers were answered. Our time together at the beach proved unbelievably good for Gabriella. She has recovered enormously."

She flattened her palm over her heart. "*Really?* That's the best news I've had in a long time."

"Yes. Amazing news," he concluded hoping that he wouldn't have to expound further on the details. Jack held her gaze. "Anything else?" he said with an air of dismissal.

Picking up the cue she said, "No. I'm thrilled that you had a good time. I'll leave you to catch up. Buzz if you need me."

The door latched behind her with a feint snap.

Jack had no intention of catching up on work. He wanted to remain home with his daughter, hovering, assuring himself that her recovery was permanent— whether she was in "magical" OBX or home with him. But his subterfuge of the fire drill leaving the Inn depended on his tending to a supposed work emergency. So he had no choice but to leave for the office first thing Monday morning.

Marooned at his desk, he wondered how Gabriella

fared with her tutor. He smiled imagining the teacher's shock when Gabriella surely greeted her verbally when their housekeeper let her in the door.

His buzzer sounded and Jack gave a start. Engaging the microphone, he responded, "Yes, Jeannie."

"Miss O'Shea on one."

Speak of the devil. He picked up the phone and pressed the line button. "Hey, Jodi. How are things going?"

Her bubbly laughter sounded. "Things *couldn't* be better. Mr. Tremonti, she doesn't need me anymore. She asked me to call."

Jack heard Gabriella's voice in the background. "OK. Put her on."

"Here's your daddy," Jodi said.

"Hi, Daddy. I asked Miss O'Shea if I could go back to school now. She said I had to ask you."

The impact of the simple request flattened his spine against the back of his chair. "Of course. Starting tomorrow. I'll call City Day School right away. Can you please pass the phone back to Miss O'Shea? I'd like another word with her."

"Sure, Daddy. Thank you."

"You're very welcome. I love you, sweetheart."

"I love you, too."

The sweet interchange rang in his ears as he waited for the phone to change hands.

"Mister Tremonti?"

He cleared his throat. "Hi again, Jodi. I'm going to call her school when we hang up, but before I do, is she behind in anything?"

"Gabriella, can you please continue reading chapter

ten while I step out of the room to talk to your dad for a minute?" Jodi directed her pupil.

A couple seconds later, Jodi said, "Based on her acing all the written tests I've administered the past six months, she should have no problem continuing with the fifth grade curriculum. I have to say, I'm thrilled for her and you. How in the world did you achieve the breakthrough?"

The magnitude of what he owed Bree and her sisters cowed him. How could he continue to rationalize his decision to leave as what's best for his daughter? "I guess we finally met the right...therapist," he said.

"Well, I'd like to meet that person, that's for sure. Despite the sadness that acquainted me with your daughter, it has been a sheer pleasure working with her. And you. All the best to you, Mister Tremonti."

"And to you, Jodi. Thank you for all you've done."

Jack hung up the phone and sat back, his hands folded over his abdomen, deep in thought. If he could just erase the whole flight of the pelicans deal from his mind.

Since Sophia's death, and even before then, during the slow death of a real marriage, Jack wanted an everyday, normal life. Quiet. Tranquil. Peaceful. Maybe fixing savory meals to relish with his family, pizza nights, helping with homework, listening to today's happenings at school, a glass of wine on the balcony, enjoying the Lake Michigan view after his girl was tucked in bed. That kind of normal.

Before his trip to North Carolina, he thought that he'd never have normal again with Gabriella. In six days, step by halting step, Gabriella's heart opened to Bree and Skye's gentle, loving touch. When it came to

Bree, so had Jack's heart.

In the middle of last night, back in his own room, he had jolted awake, panting and sweating, reliving every panic-stricken second of Gabriella's abduction. Jettisoned out of bed by the nightmare, he had run into her bedroom. She slept like an angel, a beatific smile on her lips. Returning to his bed, he lay staring at the ceiling, a waking bad dream supplanting the kidnapping scenario. Pain suffused him at the nightmare of losing Bree.

Examining his decision to leave after the fact, he still couldn't reframe his reaction to what he could only think of as witchery. How could exposure to that be good for a ten-year old girl? Or a thirty-five-year old man?

But today, that apparently unaffected ten-year-old had asked in honeyed tones to go back to school like a regular kid. How did he explain that?

****

Two weeks after their early morning departure from Norfolk, Gabriella was the only member of the Jackson Tremonti family *remotely* normal. Chirpy and smiling and uncomplaining about virtually everything, her emotional pendulum had swung so far to the extreme positive that Jack frequently worried that she was delusional.

But he knew in his heart that those worries were ungrounded. His daughter was absolutely fine. Increasingly, he suspected that his sacrificing his relationship with Bree for Gabriella's sake was deluding himself. Plagued by the blooming unrest in his heart, he struggled to recapture equilibrium. Wouldn't Doctor Breeze Layton have a heyday with diagnosing him?

He missed Bree with raw, gut stabbing intensity. Mental snapshots popped into his consciousness unbidden: her porcelain silken skin, sun-kissed on a balmy beach; emerald eyes sparkling in the moonlight; blood boiling kisses; and the soft press of her breasts against his chest as he took her into his arms. Jack longed to undo the damage he had surely left behind with his cold, abrupt departure. But the question remained, how?

****

Jack glanced across the room at Gabriella. She sat on the sofa with her legs tucked up beneath her bottom with her head bent over the book spread open in her lap. Her raven locks curtained her face. The rays of a rosy sunset through the west-facing window pane formed the backdrop behind her, a pretty picture he savored, capturing his daughter in unaware innocence.

He had always enjoyed just hanging with her. Inspired to reinstate a favorite way to hang out together he said, "I have an idea. Are you up for some Lou Malnati's?"

"Oh, yes! And cheddar cubes, too?"

"You bet. I'll call in the order. Which would you rather do: have the delivery service pick it up, or hop into a cab and go over there together?" he asked, hoping she favored the latter.

She closed her book and scrambled off the sofa. "Let's go in a cab."

Twenty minutes later, Jack slid onto a wood bench across from the take-out counter at Lou's pizzeria on Wells Street, Gabriella close beside him. He craned his neck to pan the restaurant side to side, front to back.

There were no empty stools at the bar to his left. A Blackhawks game displayed on screens suspended from the ceiling. A roar sounded as the Hawks scored a goal.

Bree lived a few blocks away. She had told Jack that she was a Friday night pizza addict, like him. Would she walk in the door and provide him with the entrée he hoped he had conjured with the cab ride over here?

"Tremonti?" the arm-tattooed teen with a ring in her nose who stood behind the counter called out.

Reluctantly Jack stepped forward, paid for his order and hoisted up the warm-bottomed, tomato, garlic and oregano scented pizza box. He accompanied Gabriella across the street, opened for her the back door of the cab idling at the curb and then slid inside the car. The driver turned onto Kinsey Street, as expected, to head back to Lake Shore Drive. Zipping through the La Salle Street intersection, Jack stared out the window, focused on the revolving door of the Sterling Building. Bree's home. Had she returned? Surely by now. But much as he hoped to catch sight of her near her home turf, he was disappointed.

Back at his condo building, he and Gabriella detoured to the bank of mailboxes. He handed her the box key, which she used, swinging open the metal door.

"Oh my gosh," she exclaimed grasping hold of a thin, rectangular package and sliding it out of the box. "I'll bet this is the video from Skye."

"Great. We can eat our pizza in the family room while we watch the video, if you want."

"I do. Let's go, Daddy. I can't wait to see Mavis and Minerva go back home."

Settled down on the couch, Jack triggered the DVD

240

to play with the remote control. He leaned over the coffee table and detached a floppy wedge of pizza from the pie, folded it in half and brought the food up to his lips. Jack took a bite and then another as the video rolled. The action panned the now familiar seascape and then Skye's beautiful face, so like Bree's, came into view, deepening Jack's sense of loss. Gabriella's eyes didn't leave the screen during the approximate half hour run time of the video. The last few frames riveted Jack's attention.

Summer and Bree posed on the sand slightly apart from the gathered crowd. They waved and Bree said, "Hi, Dad." Summer echoed the greeting.

Bree smiled directly into the camera, her pine colored eyes mesmerizing—as if gazing straight at him. Just him. *If only.*

He wanted to rewind and savor the sight again and again. Gabriella, bless her heart, read his mind.

"Can we watch it one more time?"

He was quick to respond, "Sure."

Jack regarded Bree's animated image during the second screening becoming more distraught over the fact that he had shut the woman he loved out of his life, possibly forever. What difference did it make if she could turn into a pelican or a polar bear? Did that change the fact that she was the loveliest creature inside and out that Jack had ever known?

"Daddy, you look so sad."

"I do? I'm sorry," he said trying to shake off his feeling of helplessness.

"Why are you sad?"

Confiding in a child, especially a child who had suffered more than her share of loss, might be risky.

However, Jack suspected that his child might be wise beyond her years.

"I'm sad because I think I've hurt Bree so much that there's no way for me to fix things."

"You miss her?"

"Yes. Terribly. Do you?"

"Uh huh."

"So I guess you can see why I'm sad."

She nodded her head. Doe-eyed, she gazed at him and said, "But there *is* a way to fix things."

"Yeah? How?"

"I had an idea and Skye said she would help me with it."

"What do you mean, 'Skye said'?"

"Skye talks to me all the time."

Jack knew better at that point of his tenuous acceptance of the sisters' gifts than to inquire further other than to say, "OK. What's your idea?"

Chapter 26

Rachael Johnson sashayed into Bree's office, a stack of files in her arms. "Welcome back, boss. You look horrible. I hope those bags under your eyes are the result of partying too hard."

After she dumped the files down on a chair, she skirted Bree's desk to open the blinds, unleashing a flood of sunshine into the room. "What are you doing with the blinds closed on a sunny day? After that gray winter you need to let the sunshine in every chance you have."

Winded, she plopped her ample hips into the other chair in front of Bree's cherry wood desk, a smile creasing her toffee colored cheeks.

"Good morning, Rae. I missed you." Bree smiled.

She did miss her loud, in-your-face assistant. No matter the seriousness of what Bree handled in her practice, Rae always managed to put a bright-side spin on each day. "What's new since I've been away?"

"Oh honey, you dodged some serious shit. Dr. Jameson's wife showed up and confronted Julia. She was hollering the whole time and you could hear her all the way to the emergency room. Needless to say, Julia has resigned. What a mess."

Rae cracked up, belly-laughing so hard she wheezed. She plucked a tissue out of the box on Bree's desk and dabbed under her eyes.

"I wish you could have seen Jameson's face..." She erupted in another fit of laughter.

On a hiccup catch of breath she said, "Sorry." Waving her hand in front of her face, she inhaled mightily, her size E-cup breasts heaving.

Bree couldn't help joining in with Rae's infectious laughter.

"I'm actually sorry to hear she's leaving. I like Julia," Bree said. "I'll miss her."

"Well, I'll miss her, too." All mirth disappeared from Rae's face, her lips pursed. "But you get what you deserve when you go after a married man."

Rae spoke from experience. Her life had changed drastically when her husband left her for another woman.

"Anyway, back to work." She shifted to gather the stack of files off the chair next to her.

Consulting a sheet of paper clipped to the top file she said, "Your morning is packed."

No evidence of earlier hilarity remained as Rae morphed into the efficient assistant that Bree increasingly relied on to keep the office running smoothly.

"And, um... Dr. Canavan called and asked if you would do him a favor and speak with one of his patients at noon."

"No problem. Did he send over a file?"

"Not yet. I'm sure it's on its way. Oh—but there's a baby shower at lunch in the cafeteria for Mindy."

"Mindy? I thought she wasn't due for three more months."

"You're right. But she had some spotting last week and doc ordered bed rest. So she's starting early maternity leave tomorrow."

"Darn. I wish I had known. I would have picked up something for her."

"Got you covered. I bought and wrapped an adorable diaper bag from Itzy Ritzy for you to give Mindy." Rae rose from the chair leaving the files on the edge of Bree's desk. "I heard it's the one that all the celebrities buy."

"How much do I owe you?" Bree opened her bottom drawer and grasped the handle of her purse.

"Already taken care of..." Rae patted the top folder. "My reimbursement check is in this folder. Just needs your signature."

Bree thrust the drawer closed and sat erect in her chair. "What would I do without you?"

Rae took a couple of steps toward the door and then turned to face Bree. "By the way, the feeling is mutual. Honestly, I don't know what I'd do without you, boss."

She ambled to the outer office swinging the door closed behind her.

Bree stared at the door reminiscing. Hard to believe that two years had passed since Rae had started as her assistant from her job at Lou Malnati Pizzeria. Bree had decided to forego takeout one Friday night and had eaten in the restaurant where Rae, much beloved by all patrons, worked as a waitress.

Rae had waited on Bree's table, finishing her shift by delivering Bree's uneaten pizza in a take-home box and wishing Bree goodnight. On impulse, Bree convinced her to join her in a glass of wine. One round turned into two and Rae trusted Bree enough to talk about her personal life.

Bree learned that Rae's husband had abandoned her and their son. Not only was it difficult to provide for her boy financially, the late hours at the restaurant made it difficult to supervise the pre-teen. Although Rae loved the job, the Malnati family and the regulars, she was afraid that she couldn't keep her son out of trouble.

Bree had gone through three assistants in four months for a variety of depressing reasons. She offered Rae the job on the spot and had never regretted the spontaneity for one minute since.

Bree toed off each of her high heels under the desk and wiggled her stocking encased feet. A flip-flop kind of girl who loved the sand between her toes, Bree disliked the confining shoes pinching her feet.

She missed the beach and the Inn. And she always missed her family when they were separated. For the past two weeks, a new brand of "missing" had plagued her. She had never suffered absence more since Jack took Ella and walked—no, ran—out of her life.

By now, Bree had stopped constantly checking her phone for a message from Jack, convinced that she'd never hear from again. She mourned the loss and couldn't shake the penchant to relive their time together in her mind. And her aching heart.

Only the importance of her caseload diverted her from wallowing in yearning for him. She slid the stack of files toward her, opened the first on the top and immersed in her work.

The morning flew as Bree made notations in the files.

A knock sounded and Rae opened the door poking her head through the doorframe. "Dr. Canavan's office just called and cancelled the appointment."

"Did they say why?"

"No. Just that the father has changed his mind. I told them you would be here until four if they needed you. Now you can go to the baby shower. I was just about to head down. But I'll wait for you if you want?"

"That would be great. Just let me freshen up and I'll be right with you."

Bree grabbed her purse out of her bottom drawer and entered the small private washroom in her office suite. Gazing in the mirror, she tugged the tortoise clip out of her hair and let loose a tumble of coppery curls over her shoulders. Tossing the clip into her purse that gaped open on the lip of the sink, she extracted a hair brush. She brushed the tangles out of her hair, dabbed a little concealer under her eyes and applied a touch of gloss on her lips.

Before she zipped her purse shut, she fished out her phone and slipped it into the pocket of her black maxi skirt. Bree straightened the hem of the yellow and white top trimmed with large black buttons that complemented the skirt, and deemed herself ready for the party. She locked her purse in her desk and then joined Rae in the hallway. They rode the elevator along with other office workers bound for the cafeteria.

"Obviously, Mindy is expecting a boy." Bree surveyed the room festooned with blue balloons and streamers. Flower arrangements in little blue wagons adorned tables covered with blue and white checkered cloths.

Rae piled their present in the designated place and then directed Bree to the empty table in the front of the room after they loaded plates at the buffet. Their seats faced a throne-like, high-backed armchair where Mindy would open her gifts.

"Surprise!" the assembly chorused when Mindy appeared at the entrance to the cafeteria.

The expectant mother's cheeks blushed crimson and tears streamed as she touched a hand to her chest. Deafening applause accompanied her trip to the front of the room.

Standing in front of the throne-chair Mindy gasped, "You guys are the best."

She blew her nose and shoved the crumpled tissue in her pocket. "I can't believe this."

Extending her arm straight out, she pumped it up and down and said, "Please, everyone sit."

Eying the table laden with presents, Mindy wagged her head, a wonderstruck expression on her face. She lowered down to her seat, her cheeks still flaming.

Female laughter and conversation sounded while the men in attendance seemed intent only on wolfing down a free meal. By the time Mindy finished her lunch and began opening her cache of presents, only women remained to ooh and ah over tiny outfits and footwear. Mindy displayed a teensy Green Bay Packer jersey setting off a jovial round of boos and hisses.

"Never mind, little one," Mindy said glancing down at her stomach. Raising her head, she directed a defiant smile to the room at large and said, "Go Pack."

More boos sounded as Rae went for a second slice of cake and left Bree alone at the table.

Bree checked her phone. No new messages. Satisfied that she could sit a few minutes before returning to her office to prepare for her next appointment, she set the phone on the table and leaned back in her chair, relaxed.

Suddenly, a song with a driving rock beat played through the hospital's PA speakers in the room. More familiar with tinkling lullaby music playing at the birth of babies sporadically during each day, Bree was amazed when Mindy stood up and gyrated to the music. In unison, an entire group seated at a table in the back of the room rose and joined in dancing. Consecutively, the remaining occupied tables followed suit. Flabbergasted and feeling conspicuous alone in her place, Bree, the last to stand, danced, too, scanning the room searching for Rae.

The song finished playing. Bree was half-lowered into a sitting position back in her chair when the Bruno Mars song *Marry Me* blasted through the speakers.

Bree's throat constricted and tears welled as the tune spurred memories of the flash mob at Jeanette's Pier. Unmoored, she stood upright and cast her eyes around the room to locate Rae. Mindy danced to this song, too. Unsure whether or not she should join in the dance fest, Bree continued looking for Rae.

Finally, she caught sight of her assistant standing near the cafeteria entrance flanked by two other women. Each of the trio, dangled a poster-sized, sheet of blank, white oaktag at knee level.

"Everyone…" Mindy called out, drawing Bree's attention back to front of the room.

The pregnant woman stood at attention, her right arm extended with her index finger pointing straight at the back of the room.

Bree redirected her focus again to where Mindy pointed.

The lady to Rae's right held up the poster board,

displaying the word, *Will*. Rae, beaming a smile, whipped her sign overhead, *You*. The third sign bearer revealed the word, *Marry*.

Riveted by the replay of the pier flash mob, Bree stood rooted in place, her heart pumping wildly.

Ella danced through the doorway waving a sign over her head. *Us?*

She took a place next to the rest of the sign bearers, the message unmistakably spelled out. And then Jack appeared at the entrance. Bree's breath caught in her throat as her jaw dropped.

Jack scanned the room until his eyes met hers. His lips curled into a sexy smile. Paralyzed, Bree gaped at him, her eyes frozen wide open in disbelief.

Ella tossed down her sign and raced toward Bree. She wrapped her arms around Bree's hips and squeezed. Arching her neck, she looked up at Bree. "It was my idea and Skye helped me," she said sweetly.

She heard Ella's voice clearly, but the language didn't register in her consciousness. Jack was all Bree saw. That he had come to her, was all Bree knew.

He drew nearer in seeming slow motion. As if dreaming, she followed his progress with hungry eyes, the yearned for sight of him healing what was broken inside. Ella loosened her embrace and side stepped, making way for her father. Jack halted directly in front of Bree and slowly lowered to one knee as the music stopped.

Bree whipped her hand over her mouth, awestricken, her heart pounding.

Jack's gray eyes met hers, penetrating, transfixing. "Oh my God, Jack…"

He winked. "Hey, it worked for the guy at the

pier."

Jack enveloped her hands in his, warming her when she had felt so cold without him. "Bree, forgive me for the way I left. For my inaction the past couple weeks. I didn't know how to fix things. I…"

Jack heaved a breath and then continued, "I was a fool to think we could live without you. That you could be anything but good in our lives. From the day I met you, it was written in the stars that we should be together. I have missed you more than I ever thought possible. I don't want to spend another day without you in my life."

He let loose his right hand, reached out and clasped Ella's hand. "We don't want to live another day without you."

Ella beamed a gleeful smile at Bree. "Daddy. Show her the box!"

The chattering cafeteria crowd hemmed in Bree, Jack and Ella. Too shocked to feel self-conscious at the center of attention, Bree stood tethered to one of Jack's hands. He stuffed his other hand into his jacket.

The small jewelry box that he brought into view had Bree choking back a sob. This moment. This man. Every girlhood fantasy fulfilled. With a snap, Jack opened the box revealing a glittering, heart-shaped solitaire ring perched on a velvet cushion.

Tears flowed as Bree's vision narrowed, blurring everything and everyone but Jack. She couldn't tell which of them was shaking, or maybe both. His eyes soft, earnest, he said, "Bree will you make me the happiest man on earth? Will you please marry us?"

She searched his eyes for any whisper of doubt. No matter how much she wanted to accept his proposal, he had to accept *all* of her. "Are you sure, Jack?" Her voice cracked.

"I have never been more sure of anything in my life."

"Triplets and all?"

He grinned. "I love kids," he said rising to his feet and embracing her.

Tilting back her head within the circle of his arms she cried, "Then yes. Yes! I'll marry you!"

His lips found hers and the room erupted in cheers. Jack slipped the pretty ring on her finger—a perfect fit. Ella hopped up and down yelling, "Yay!"

Jack swung first Bree and then Ella around in a circle. He set his daughter on her feet and Bree stooped to gather Ella in a warm hug.

"Do you like your ring, Bree? I helped pick it out."

"I love it. It's perfect."

A mosquito buzz sounded and Bree glanced at her phone vibrating on the table. Picking up the device she squinted at the text message icon displaying a tiny number three. Identical texts from Mom, Skye and Summer read, SAY YES!!!

She dashed off three identical replies, *I just did!*

A word about the author...

K.M. Daughters is the penname for team writers and sisters, Pat Casiello and Kathie Clare. The penname is dedicated to the memory of their parents, "K"ay and "M"ickey Lynch. K.M. Daughters is the author of thirteen award winning fiction novels. The "Daughters" are wives, mothers and grandmothers residing in the Chicago suburbs and on the Outer Banks, North Carolina. Visitors are most welcome at http://www.kmdaughters.com

Thank you for purchasing
this publication of The Wild Rose Press, Inc.

For questions or more information
contact us at
info@thewildrosepress.com.

The Wild Rose Press, Inc.
www.thewildrosepress.com

To visit with authors of
The Wild Rose Press, Inc.
join our yahoo loop at
http://groups.yahoo.com/group/thewildrosepress/

CPSIA information can be obtained
at www.ICGtesting.com
Printed in the USA
BVHW031135111022
649147BV00014B/1141